DEPTHS OF BETRAYAL

THE SOUL BOUND SAGA
BOOK THREE

JAMES E WISHER

SAND HILL PUBLISHING

Edited by: Janie Linn Dullard

Cover art by: B-Ro

ISBN: 978-1-68520-031-2

010120231.0

CHAPTER 1

Joran Den Cade blinked exhausted eyes and tried to focus on the imperial palace looming directly ahead of him. On his left rode the Iron Princess, Alexandra Tiberius, member of the imperial family and his fiancée. On his right rode Mia Amino, his soulmate, adopted sister, and the most important person in the world to him. Neither of them looked half as exhausted as he felt. No surprise there. Mia had spent years training to be a warrior and Alexandra would have been beautiful no matter how tired she felt. Joran hated to use any of the substances he kept in his alchemist's kit, but right now a little stimulant wouldn't go wrong.

At least the sun felt warm on his shoulders. It would have been a beautiful autumn day if not for the small number of zombies still wandering the countryside, the—he knew not how many—mysteries he had to unravel, and the fact that Princess Alexandra insisted they report in to her father, the emperor, immediately on arrival. When you thought about it, exhaustion was the natural response to everything he had to deal with.

They'd left the bulk of the Second Legion to hunt down any zombie stragglers and returned to Tiber with a modest escort of Iron Guards. Happily, they hadn't run into anything or anyone that wanted to kill them on the three-day trip. That many days without a violent encounter of some sort came close to a recent record.

He took a deep breath of the crisp air and offered a silent prayer to The One God that they'd have a chance to at least wash up, change clothes, and get a cup of tea. Strong tea, with lots of honey.

"Copper for your thoughts," Mia said.

Joran offered a wan smile. "I'm praying for a cup of tea, and a nap wouldn't go amiss."

"Oh, I figured you were thinking about those weird chambers we found under Fort Death."

He grimaced. The chambers in question appeared to be where the zombies they'd fought had been created by whoever controlled them. They'd found nothing in the way of instructions or notes and the simple stone slabs revealed no secrets. All in all, they'd left with many more questions than answers.

"They were the least interesting thing down there. Empty workshops devoid of everything save frustration. Pity whoever worked there didn't leave a journal behind, but I suppose that would've been too much to ask for. The best thing the army could do is collapse those caverns—fort and all—then rebuild somewhere else. Not sure if they will or not, but that's beyond my control."

"Are you going to be okay?" Mia's concern came loud and clear through their link.

"I will. A hot meal and a good night's sleep in a proper bed will set things right. I've completely lost track of how long we've been going nonstop. It's amazing you're not more tired than me. You did all the actual fighting after all."

"I'm used to it. In the city guard, we sometimes worked twenty-four hours straight. Not often, thank The One God, but when it happened, I thought the day would never end."

Alexandra led them around to the side entrance near her suite and the three of them dismounted. "Tend the horses. I don't know how long our meeting with Father will take, but I doubt we'll be heading out again today."

"Yes, Majesty," the leader of the Iron Guard unit said.

"Any chance of a rest before we meet with the emperor?" Joran asked. His voice sounded entirely too pathetic in his own ears.

"Yes. If we show up looking like this, I'll never hear the end of it. Besides, I want him to have a chance to calm down before we talk. I did sort of ignore a direct order not to take command of the legion. Father hates it when I do things like that." Alexandra yanked the door open and they followed her inside.

Joran smiled at the soft carpet under his feet. Back in civilization at last.

"Do you often ignore his orders?" Mia asked.

"Not the important ones." Alexandra pushed through the suite doors and a moment later her six servants came boiling out of the back room. "The problem is, Father and I sometimes disagree about which ones are the important ones."

"I imagine the emperor thinks all of them are important," Joran said.

"Exactly! He's completely unreasonable sometimes. How many whorehouses do you think we'd have had to search to find General Artum? We didn't have time for that sort of foolishness. Speaking of the general, I'm going to have to think up a good punishment for him." Alexandra shook her head and turned toward her room. Glancing back over her shoulder she added, "You've got an hour, then we see Father."

Joran glanced at the two servants—Marsa and one whose name escaped him—that had been designated for his use. "Whatever she's drinking to get that much energy, I want some."

The servants giggled and Marsa said, "I think Her Majesty's energy comes from inside. But I can get you a nice snack."

"The One God bless you. Hot tea if you can find it as well, please."

When Marsa smiled and headed for the kitchen the second girl said, "I'll fetch you a clean robe, my lord."

Joran and Mia retreated to the room they shared. Inside, Joran went to the pitcher of water, poured a bowl full, and splashed his face. The chill water did wonders to wake him up.

"Do you suppose the servants think it's strange that you and I share a room instead of you and Alexandra?"

Joran pulled off his filthy tunic and tossed it in the bin. "I doubt they worry about our sleeping arrangements. They know we're soulmates, so our staying close shouldn't surprise them. As for Alexandra and I, we're only engaged. If our sleeping situation stays the same after the wedding, then they'll have something to talk about.

The meeting with Joran's future father-in-law thankfully didn't take place in the rather intimidating throne room. Instead, they ended up in some sort of salon decorated with far too much crimson and gold silk. A faint, spicy incense filled the air. He didn't recognize the scent, so the palace hadn't bought it from Den Cade Trading.

Joran fought back a sneeze and tried to look calmer than he felt. His meal and sugary tea had given him a burst of energy. Nothing that would last, but hopefully enough to get him through the meeting.

The overstuffed chair where the emperor waited rested in the middle of the room and, when you combined his posture with his purple robe of state, it might as well have been the eagle throne. His dark eyes bore into them with such intensity Joran feared he might burst into flames.

If her father's obvious displeasure bothered Alexandra, she gave no sign. Perhaps familiarity reduced the impact. Maybe if he lived another hundred years it would cease to trouble him as well.

Joran took some small comfort from the presence of the much more relaxed crown prince. Marcus dressed in soft gray robes and silk slippers. He looked very much like a man recently risen and in need of a mug of mulled wine. Joran would have liked something far stronger.

The emperor leaned forward and stared at Alexandra. "Were my orders unclear? I said you were not to assume command of the Second Legion, yet that's exactly what you did. How can I expect my subjects to obey me when my own daughter doesn't?"

Alexandra cocked her head. "Didn't Marcus give you my message? General Artum left the palace grounds for some fun in the city. Since a small army of monsters was wandering the countryside, I made the decision to take his place. I didn't think you'd want me to wait until he came back, especially given the circumstances. Did I err in my judgement?"

The emperor ground his teeth. "No, but from now on you'll do as you're told."

"Of course, Father," she said in a tone that made it clear she had no intention of doing as she was told. "Should we give our report now?"

"Please do."

Alexandra looked at Joran. Of course "we" naturally meant him. He took a step closer to the emperor, cleared his throat, and recounted everything that had happened since they left the throne room nearly a week ago. The emperor's eyes widened when he reached the part about the bile spring apparently being constructed rather than natural, but other than that he gave away nothing.

When Joran finished Alexandra stepped in. "We believe the next step is for Joran to continue his investigation in the Forbidden Section of the library. I doubt the church would accept anything less than your command to allow him access."

The emperor finally leaned back and rubbed his eyes. For a moment, Joran saw signs of the toll his near death by poison had taken. Despite its power, even a cure all wasn't an absolute miracle. That sort of stress had to take something out of a man and the emperor wasn't as young as he used to be. Hopefully the strain of the current crisis wouldn't be too much for him to bear.

"Is there no other avenue you can pursue?" the emperor asked at last.

"No, Father," Alexandra said, her voice having lost some of its stridency. Perhaps she saw the stress on his face as well. "Every other line of inquiry has hit a brick wall. If the Forbidden Section doesn't yield some clue about our next move, we'll be reduced to waiting for the enemy to attack and reacting. I don't know about you, but I've had enough of reacting."

"So be it." The emperor's expression hardened, all signs of weakness gone as quickly as they appeared. "I'll have the scribes draw something up and sign it in the morning. I'd been hoping to avoid a conflict with the church, but it seems our options are limited. If the fight must be had, best we have it now, before the next crisis hits."

The emperor dismissed them and the trio set out for Alexandra's suite.

"That went pretty well, considering," Mia said.

"Father knows as well as I do that obeying orders is a fine thing, but in an emergency, sometimes you have to do the right thing rather than what you're supposed to."

"Is that what you tell the generals?" Joran asked.

"Ha! I would if those fools ever did anything right. I still have to think up a punishment for General Artum."

"How hard is that?" Mia asked. "Dereliction of duty usually gets ten lashes for a first offense."

"Somehow I doubt generals receive the same punishment as a common legionnaire," Joran said.

"Exactly." Alexandra ran her fingers through her short, dark hair. "In addition to their high posts in the military, most of the generals are also prominent members of the nobility. Artum is the brother of the current head of the Den Rodius family. As nobles go, not the most powerful, but they do control some of our most productive iron mines. If they get angry, a slowdown in production might make things difficult for the army. I think a demotion to logistics will be in order. I'll stick him in an office somewhere, let him sign paperwork, and keep him out of the way."

"Joran, the paperwork," Mia said. "Remember, you wanted to check on it."

That's right. He'd been so tired it completely slipped his mind. "Do you know who the commander of Fort Death reported to?"

Alexandra pushed through the door to the suite and dropped into her favorite spot on the couch. "No, but I can find out. Why?"

"Well, from the looks of it, the fort had been compromised for months. I'm assuming that someone should have noticed that the reports had stopped. And if they didn't pass that information up the chain of command, either they're incompetent or working for the enemy."

Alexandra closed her eyes and blew out a sigh. "I'll look into it. You just focus on your research. The less time you spend in the Forbidden Section, the better for everyone."

Joran would happily drink to that plan. "Then I'd best get my questions ready. If you'll excuse me."

He retreated to his bedroom and quickly collected Samaritan's workbook. Joran needed to finish reading it before he left. If, The One God forbid, he found anything that confirmed Samaritan's claims about alchemy being just another way to manipulate the energy field he called the ether, it might change everything about their understanding of magic and possibly The One God himself.

CHAPTER 2

The archbishop—Fane smiled when she thought of herself that way—walked along the dark, silent halls of her citadel. So many of the fools that joined the cult imagined she'd discovered some make-believe deity like the Church of The One God. Others, those of higher rank, believed knowledge was The One True God. They were closer to the truth.

Her master, Amet Sur, had taught her, long before she and the other arcane lords' apprentices followed their masters to this miserable world, that the only thing worth worshipping was power. Seek it out, control it, and let nothing stand in your way. Fane had cast away her humanity in her quest for power. Her new, undead body served far better than her weak mortal form ever had.

Unfortunately, it drew far too much attention whenever she left the citadel. It also had certain vulnerabilities that made travel during daylight hours a dubious proposition. That forced her to rely on lesser servants. Fane rounded a corner and descended a set of stairs that led to the citadel basement.

She'd created many servants in the centuries since her master returned to their home world. Some, like the overseers, had turned out reasonably well. Others had ended up in the pit of rejects. The best part about an immortal body was the unlimited time she had to experiment. Even so, she never took her glowing red eyes off the mission her master had given her before he departed.

He'd said this world held a hidden source of astonishing corrupt power. Her master had then ordered her to find that power source and seize it. Doubtless the other arcane lords had given their own apprentices the same order, but they had all died long ago. Now the power would be hers alone.

Three centuries of study and research finally revealed the source of the corruption her master sensed: a dragon of immeasurable power slept somewhere on this world. Even a creature the size of a dragon had little trouble hiding when you compared it to the entire world.

Fane set her musings aside and stopped in front of the chamber where one of her most successful experiments waited. The mist wraith had taken a decade to perfect and she'd only created one. She opened the door and immediately a chill breeze filled with delicious corruption swirling around her.

A fang-filled smile creased her face. "Wraith. I have a mission for you."

The breeze took on the physical form of a cloaked humanoid. "I am at your service, Mistress."

"One of my idiot overseers has lost a valuable artifact, one of the four black iron swords my master provided before his departure. It's entirely too valuable to leave in the hands of our enemies, not that the fools could even use it. Retrieve the sword and bring it back here."

"As you command, Mistress. Do you wish me to use stealth or are casualties acceptable?"

"I don't care if you have to kill everyone in the miserable empire. Just get my sword."

Wraith lowered its head. "Yes, Mistress."

She stepped out of the doorway. Wraith vanished and a corrupt breeze caressed her before it vanished. She really shouldn't let the creature get away with such familiarity, yet its touch sent a pleasant thrill through her twisted soul. She shut the door and resumed her walk.

So much remained to be done and she had so few reliable servants.

A faint ripple ran through the ether before touching her mind. Speaking of servants, here was one now.

Fane closed her eyes and concentrated, following the ripple back to its source. Her psychic self raced northwest before diving underground. She ended up in a small stone chamber where a single dwarf sat cross-legged, holding an amulet engraved with the slashed circle of the cult. She shook her intangible head. The church's symbol with a line through it, how did they ever convince anyone with such a simple design?

"You have news?" she asked.

"Yes, Archbishop. The human, Samaritan, has arrived at our base. He wishes to begin the search soon."

"Good. Provide him with whatever help he requires and be sure to keep a keen lookout for anything that might indicate where the capital of the ancient empire might be hidden."

"Do you wish him to succeed in activating the weapon?" the dwarf asked.

"I couldn't possibly care less. If he does and the dwarven province is destroyed or weakened, fine. I assume you and the other rebels will be quick to pick up the pieces and take over."

"If it pleases you, Archbishop, we will. The empire and its church have destroyed our once-thriving culture. All the dwarves care about now is—"

She ended the conversation and returned her awareness to her body. Fane cared nothing for the causes of those who joined the cult. They were all using each other and only the stupidest or most blindly devout believed otherwise. None of it mattered. Once she woke the dragon and seized control of its power, this world would be hers to rule until her master returned.

Even the mighty Amet Sur would have to praise her when she handed him an entire world.

———

Samaritan shivered and huddled closer to the glowing rocks that served as a heat source in his quarters. Quarters being a generous description for a cave dug into the side of a mountain. He had no furniture beyond a patch of moss that they said would serve as a bed. Samaritan had lived rough plenty of times, but this arrangement pushed his tolerance to the limit. Who would have guessed a tent provided by the lizardmen wouldn't be the worst of his accommodations? He shuddered to think where he might end up next on his quest for revenge.

As for his hosts, the so-called dwarven cultists turned out to be a rebel band that sought to kick the empire out of their territory and kill the imperial loyalists that ruled the province. If The One True God cult would help in their mission, they'd happily say whatever they had to in order to gain access to the resources they needed. He couldn't exactly find fault since he used the cult in exactly the same way.

No, true believers they weren't. Not that Samaritan had much in the way of faith remaining in him. True faith, he'd learned, was in far shorter supply in the world than he'd imagined when he still served as a White Knight. He'd been so naive back then. Looking back, his younger self disgusted him.

He straightened and stepped out into the tunnel connecting his cave to the main gathering area where the rest of the rebels congregated on more patches of moss. Forty dwarves didn't make the most impressive army and the less said about the smell of mushrooms roasting on heated stones, the better. There were supposed to be other groups scattered here and there, but the archbishop only had allies in this one.

Or so she claimed. Samaritan took everything she told him with a grain of salt.

One of the dwarves stood and stomped over to him. When he got closer, Samaritan recognized Grub. It seemed he'd drawn the short straw and gotten stuck dealing with their too-tall guest.

"Need something, human?"

"I wondered if you had a map of the underground, and a meal wouldn't go amiss."

"Maps are worthless down here. Tunnels collapse and fissures open all the time. Any map we made would be out of date in a year. Tell me what you're looking for and I'll try my best to show you where to find it. As for food, you can help yourself to roasted shrooms."

Dinner would keep. He needed to try and figure out where the second beast slept. "Are there any ancient manmade tunnels? Perhaps leading to a lava pit?"

Grub scratched his beard. "All the tunnels around here are dwarfmade. Humans digging this deep is asking for trouble. I do know a couple places where lava bubbles up, but it's not a lake of the stuff. More like cracks where it oozes out."

Samaritan frowned. Not exactly an auspicious start to his search. "My research indicates an ancient empire ruled this continent about six hundred or so years ago. Do you have any records from that time?"

Grub waved a dismissive hand. "What you see is what we've got. Any records are kept in the capital. And no one there's going to let one of us look around, much less a human."

His frown smoothed. Maybe not any human, but for an imperial noble in good standing, perhaps an exception could be made. And Samaritan knew just which noble might help him.

CHAPTER 3

I t took Joran until nearly midnight to fully read and absorb the information in Samaritan's workbook. For the sake of the empire, he dearly hoped the man wrote from a place of madness rather than fact. That said, some of the concepts, even touched on briefly as they were, fascinated him. Not that he would ever admit that out loud, but the idea of the ether and being able to manipulate it directly and so affect reality without the need for complex potions appealed to him a great deal.

The more pressing concern at the moment focused on an empire that existed long before the birth of the first Marcus Tiberius. The few details he found indicated they'd ruled an area vastly larger than the Tiberian Empire and they kept their enemies at bay using a variety of magics. One of which, the one that seemed to interest Samaritan, focused on manipulating living things to turn them into weapons. The serpent being the pinnacle of that art. And from the sounds of it, three more just as bad lurked out there somewhere.

They needed to find them before Samaritan set them loose to do The One God only knew how much damage.

And so Joran found himself trudging across the dew-covered grass of the palace grounds toward the college far too early in the morning. He clutched the imperial writ in his right hand. A messenger had delivered it to Alexandra's suite at dawn this morning. He didn't need direct orders to know that he needed to get going as soon as possible.

Beside him, Mia looked no happier about their situation. She'd developed a considerable dislike for the library after their earlier attempts at research. No doubt visions of dry texts waiting to lull her to sleep danced in her imagination.

"Perhaps the books in the Forbidden Section will be more interesting than the ones we read last time," Joran said.

Mia snorted. "What do you want to bet?"

He smiled. "Nothing, I'm just trying to cheer you up. Sometimes I wonder if there's a class I missed on making technical and historical texts as boring as possible. I've read plenty of them over the years and I can count on both hands the number where I actually enjoyed the presentation of the information as much as the knowledge itself. Don't worry. If you want to take a nap, I'll do the actual research."

"No, much as I'd like to take you up on that offer, I'll do my best to help. Maybe if you gave me some specific words to look for, I could scan through the text while you do a deeper dive."

"That might work. I've never actually tried doing research that way. Probably because I always did this sort of thing on my own."

"Well, you're not on your own now, so let's do this. I want to find Samaritan and introduce him to my sword."

Joran dearly hoped she got the chance. The man struck him

as far too dangerous and obsessed to be left wandering the empire causing trouble.

The rest of the walk went quickly and they soon were standing in front of the library doors, only a minute after they opened. Joran looked up at the gray stone-and-glass building. Why had he never noticed how much it resembled a church? The thought did nothing to ease his nerves.

Taking a deep breath, he led the way up a short flight of steps and opened the door for Mia. Inside, he went right up the central aisle toward the desk where the librarian and his assistants worked to keep the thousands of books in order. A small silver bell sat on the edge of the desk for those occasions when everyone had other things to do.

To his considerable relief, Julian stood behind the desk this morning, sparing him the need to deal with a stranger. The fewer people that knew about his trip to the Forbidden Section the better.

As soon as Julian spotted them, he smiled. That smile wouldn't last long.

"Morning, Julian. I fear I have bad news." Joran held out the imperial writ. "I need access to the Forbidden Section."

Julian looked all around. "That's a bad idea, Joran. I told you, the church hates it when people go in there. I don't think anyone has even tried since I started working here."

"I believe you, my friend. Unfortunately, as you suggested last time I mentioned it, I'm completely out of options. The empire is in too much danger for me not to do everything possible to stop it."

"Okay, but I don't have the key. I'll go get Master Modius, he's the head librarian. Wait here." Julian slipped out a door behind the desk Joran hadn't even noticed.

"Where does he think we're going to go?" Mia asked.

"Julian's just nervous. Hell, I'm nervous, I just have more practice hiding it."

Mia shook her head. "I can't imagine what kind of books they have hidden back there that they go to such lengths to keep people from reading them. If the information is that dangerous, why don't they burn it or hide it in the church basement or something?"

"Burning it would be too drastic. However dangerous the information is, it might also be the key to saving the empire one day and if they burned it, the knowledge would be lost forever. Hiding it makes more sense, but then it can't serve as bait."

"Bait?"

"Sure, the church will doubtless hear about anyone who tries to gain access, even those without an imperial writ. The ones less well connected than us will almost certainly enjoy a long conversation with the inquisitors. And if they don't like what they hear..."

Joran let the rest remain unspoken as the most obese man he'd ever seen came waddling out of the back room. It astonished Joran that the head librarian even fit through the doorway. As it was, the sides of his crimson robe brushed the casing.

Sweat soaked his robe from the short walk and a deep scowl made dozens of wrinkles in his flabby face. "What's this foolishness about visiting the Forbidden Section? If you leave right now, I won't call the Inquisition."

Joran placed the writ down on the desk, making sure the eagle seal faced toward Modius. "Do you truly wish me to return and tell His Imperial Majesty that his writ is insufficient to gain access to anything he wishes? While I'm not entirely sure what his reaction might be, I'm sure you can guess."

If possible, Modius's face had gotten even redder as Joran spoke. With a trembling hand the head librarian picked up the scroll and broke the seal. A variety of facial twitches provided clues to his thoughts as he read. Joran had read the scroll himself, but when Modius lowered the scroll his face had gone from beet red to corpse white.

"Please... Please don't tell his most generous Majesty what I said. It's the church, you understand. They impressed upon me how vital it was that no one enter that section. I wouldn't dream of doing anything the emperor might consider disloyal. I'm an imperial citizen, born and raised in Tiber. You'll tell him I did as he commanded, won't you?"

"Of course I will." Joran spoke in the soft, soothing voice generally reserved for his nephews. "Now, how about we take a little walk over there and you can let us in?"

Modius reached into a pocket and pulled out a foot-long key that looked like it was made of imperial steel. "Julian is my finest assistant; he'll see that you have everything you need."

"You want me to unlock it?" Julian's voice came out in a not terribly masculine squeak.

"Yes, that's a good fellow." Modius held out the key and Julian took it with a trembling hand.

The head librarian waddled back into his office; at least that's what Joran assumed lay behind the closed door.

"How did I get dragged into this? I'm just an assistant."

"Relax," Joran said. "All you have to do is turn the key. As soon as the door is open, you can run to the farthest corner of the library. We, on the other hand, are going to search for information about a—"

"I don't want to know! This way." Julian nearly sprinted away from the desk deeper into the library.

"And I thought you were nervous," Mia said. "Will he be okay?"

"I expect. Come on, if we make him wait, he's liable to faint."

Mia let out a little giggle and they set out. He found he quite liked it when she did that. It made her sound her actual age. Sometimes, when she got really serious, she seemed far older and harder than a twenty-two-year-old woman should be. Joran resolved to make her laugh as often as possible.

They caught up with Julian at the end of a hall Joran had never explored before. It had no other rooms along it and no branches. It ended at a heavy wooden door marked with The One God's circle. Julian inserted the key into the lock, turned it two full revolutions, and pushed the door open.

As soon as he pulled the key out, Julian said, "Best of luck."

And with that he took his leave.

Joran shared a look with Mia who shrugged. Beyond the door waited a room remarkable only for its lack of remarkableness. In fact, the Forbidden Section might as well have been any other section of the library. Joran counted eight nearly full bookcases. In the center sat a perfectly ordinary table surrounded by four chairs. An alchemical light hanging from the ceiling, shed a warm, welcoming glow. Someone had to come here regularly as no dust lingered anywhere.

"This is underwhelming," Mia said. "I expected something more ominous. Compared to some of the places we've visited lately, this is actually kind of nice."

"If we can find some useful information, it'll be nicer yet."

C ardinal Rufious scratched out the line he'd just written and grimaced. He hated writing letters of condolence, but when one of the church's biggest donors died, you had to make the effort in the hope that his heirs would be equally generous. Not that he didn't want to comfort the grieving widow, but the eldest son held the purse strings. Rufious hadn't met the man personally, but the report submitted by the deacon that oversaw the late father's final days made him out to be tightfisted with his coins.

He collected a clean sheet of paper and dipped his quill. Third time lucky. An instant before the tip touched paper, someone knocked on his door. A blob of black ink splattered all over the fresh sheet of paper. Maybe not so lucky after all.

Rufious put the quill away. "Enter."

The door opened on silent, well-oiled hinges. Rufious hated squeaky doors or windows or children for that matter. A hesitant, pale-faced youth peeked in. Dressed all in white save for a black collar, the messenger boy couldn't have been more than fourteen. The youths seldom came this deep into the church. One of the underpriests should have dealt with him.

"Message, Your Grace."

"You should have brought it to the father on duty."

"I did, sir. He said you needed to see it."

"Oh. Well, bring it here."

The boy scurried over, held out a rolled-up scroll with a broken seal, and lowered his gaze to the floor. Everyone acted like they feared he might eat them whole. He didn't think he had a particularly fearsome look or reputation.

He shrugged and took the scroll. "You may go."

The messenger bowed and fled as fast as his legs would carry him.

As soon as the door closed, Rufious unrolled the scroll. Now, what was so important that the duty priest saw fit to interrupt him?

A sentence in, his eyes widened. Two people had come to the library with an imperial writ granting them access to the Forbidden Section. With everything going on with the traitor Bellator, this had to be more bad news. They needed to know what so interested the palace that the emperor himself would get involved.

Rufious pulled a rope near his desk and in the distance a bell rang. Less than a minute later a far older and more reliable messenger entered his office and bowed. "Your Grace?"

"Fetch me a squad of White Knights."

The messenger bowed and withdrew without asking any questions. That, of course, was what made the man so trustworthy, a distinct lack of curiosity combined with twenty years of loyal service.

The White Knights needed fifteen minutes to make the walk from their barracks to his office. The four men, dressed in white cloaks marked with The One God's circle over mail armor, stood facing him, hands clasped behind their backs. They all had the bronze complexion and dark hair of true imperials, though he doubted any of them were noble. Members of the nobility seldom joined the White Knights.

He grimaced. In truth, the only noble he could remember joining was Bellator and that hadn't turned out very well.

He shook his head and focused on the problem at hand. "Gentlemen, a man and a woman have entered the Forbidden Section of the library on the emperor's orders. Bring the man in for questioning. Quietly, if you please."

"You wish him undamaged, Your Grace?" the eldest knight asked.

"That would be best since he serves the emperor directly. We don't want a fight with the palace right now. As long as he's unharmed, we can claim a simple misunderstanding."

"Understood. And the woman?"

"Irrelevant. I'll meet you in interrogation room one."

The four knights bowed as one, turned on their heels, and strode out. They wouldn't fail him and Rufious would soon get to the bottom of this matter. The church didn't call it the Forbidden Section for nothing. Time for the palace to be reminded that they *needed* permission, they didn't grant it.

CHAPTER 4

Joran stood in front of a bookcase and scanned the spines of the books. Many of them were blank and the few that weren't often only had the author's name at the base and no description of the contents. He'd hoped to find a catalogue with at least a listing of the books by subject. Disappointment seemed to be his fate lately. If he had to read every book it would take forever on his own.

He glanced at Mia and smiled. She'd settled in at the room's sole desk and promptly fell asleep halfway through the book he'd given her. Perfectly expected, unlike the missing filing system. Forbidden Section or not, without help, he'd never make heads or tails of the collection.

Back at the first bookcase he pulled the thick, leather-bound volume from the top shelf. Maybe there was a way to quickly at least come to grips with the mass of volumes. He took out his workbook and opened it to a blank page. A sealed ink pot and quill came out next. The first page indicated that the book covered the names and descriptions of a variety of demons. Not what he wanted at the moment.

He made a note and replaced the book. Joran repeated the process twenty times before coming to something interesting. It seemed a thousand or so years ago, the dwarves had been enslaved and forced to work as miners for something called the Black Iron Empire. None of that meant anything to Joran, but the timeframe sounded about right. That might be the ancient empire he sought.

After all, how many ancient empires could there be?

He made a note and set the book aside for closer study. Mia muttered in her sleep and he brushed some hair out of her eyes. She always looked so much younger when she slept.

Leaving his soulmate to her nap, he returned to the bookcase. He'd only checked one shelf so far. Maybe he'd get lucky and more information about the Black Iron Empire would be in the same general area.

A soft breeze from behind him provided the only warning. The next thing Joran knew, something went over his head and the world went dark and silent.

"Help!" No reaction.

His rational mind understood that an alchemically treated bag designed to keep a prisoner blind and deaf had been placed over his head. The irrational panicked when strong hands bound his arms and grabbed his ankles, lifting him like so much baggage and whisking him The One God alone knew where.

The twisting and flexing of his body along with a barely noticeable breeze on his arms as his captors bore him along gave the only clue that he was moving. Mia's panic mingled with his own and it took every drop of self-control he possessed not to lose it. As best he could, he tried to picture Alexandra and send the idea to find her and tell her what had happened.

Joran had every confidence Mia knew exactly what to do.

A moment later she vanished from his mind.

His stomach churned and he nearly retched. His clear thoughts became muddy and he barely kept from fainting. They'd moved beyond the range of the soul bond.

Joran was on his own now.

———

J oran's blast of fear and panic had Mia awake and on her feet before she fully understood the danger. Her mind cleared in moments as she spun in time to see four figures in white carrying him through a door that had been hidden behind one of the bookcases.

She drew her sword and took three steps before the door slammed in her face.

"No! Joran!" She hurled books off the shelves in a desperate search for a switch or button or something that would let her follow the kidnappers and rescue her soulmate.

Of course, she found nothing. As she drew back to pound on the door with the pommel of her sword, an image appeared in her mind. It was Alexandra in full Iron Princess garb.

He'd sent it to her of course. Even kidnapped, Joran's mind worked better than hers. When she told the princess that White Knights had kidnapped Joran, she'd do whatever she had to in order to set him free.

Her vision went blurry and her sword felt twice as heavy. Exhaustion unlike anything she'd ever known filled her. It took only an instant for Mia to understand what had happened. Joran had moved beyond the range of their link. This was what he'd warned her about if they were separated.

Right now, she doubted she'd win a fight with a trainee to

say nothing of a full legionnaire. But Mia didn't need to fight, at least not that way.

She took a step toward the exit, paused, and turned to collect Joran's kit and workbook. He wouldn't want those left where anyone might look through them. But by The One God, did they have to be so heavy?

Shouldering the kit, she set off at a weary trudge. No one troubled her as she walked down the hall toward the main part of the library. And thank goodness for that. Mia had no strength to spare for conversation.

"Is everything okay?" Joran's friend—Mia's addled brain refused to yield his name—came her way from behind one of the bookcases.

Mia didn't slow. "No."

"Where's Joran?"

"By now likely talking to the inquisitors. If you value your life, I recommend taking the rest of the day off. When the princess gets here, she's liable to be in a poor mood."

He had nothing more to say after that, thank goodness.

She left the well-meaning man behind and shuffled out of the library. The palace seemed awfully far away all of a sudden. Especially since everything in her screamed to turn around and keep searching for Joran. She fought that instinct and kept moving. Nothing she could do on her own would save him. Only Alexandra had the authority to do what had to be done.

Time meant little to Mia. It took all her concentration to put one foot in front of the other. After an interminable journey she reached the palace and the side entrance they used to get to Alexandra's suite. Everyone knew her well enough now that they made no comment as she trudged through the halls. Just as well since she had nothing to say to anyone save the princess.

Mia sent a silent prayer heavenward that Alexandra would be waiting in her room.

Her legs were barely moving when she reached the suite door. She stumbled and bumped her head on it.

Someone inside must have thought she knocked as the door opened a moment later and a wide-eyed servant stared at her.

"Where's Lord Den Cade?"

"Alexandra?" Mia asked.

"Her Majesty is taking a nap."

"Wake her up."

The servant backed up a step. "I can't."

Mia mustered her best glare. "Wake. Her. Up!"

The servant looked like a mouse caught between a cat and a long drop to the ocean. Something in Mia's expression or maybe Joran's absence convinced her to hurry across the suite and knock on the princess's bedroom door.

Mia dragged herself into the room and dropped into an empty chair. One time she'd gotten a really bad fever and ended up so sick she couldn't get out of bed for a week. She felt worse than that now. Joran warned her what would happened if they were separated, but all the warnings in the world wouldn't have prepared her for this.

At last, the bedroom door opened and Alexandra emerged wrapped in a crimson robe. Her face resembled a storm cloud about to loose a bolt of lightning. She took one look at Mia and immediately hurried over. The servant, bless her, made herself scarce.

"Where's Joran?" Alexandra asked.

"Taken. Kidnapped by White Knights. There was a secret door in the Forbidden Section. I tried to smash it down, but failed." That explanation took so much out of her she nearly passed out.

"The church dares to kidnap someone acting under Father's personal writ? Clearly they have an overblown sense of their importance. An example will have to be made. I have a few arrangements to make. You rest. When I'm done, we'll get him back together."

That sounded like the finest thing Mia had ever heard.

———

Cardinal Rufious stood, hands clasped behind his back, and waited in the small stone chamber that served the Inquisition as an interrogation room. A red alchemical lamp tinted everything an unsettling hue. He'd chosen number one since it lacked many of the more aggressive tools of the trade. Anyone acting under the emperor's direct orders had to be important and thus needed to be treated with care.

Intimidation rather than torture would do the trick. Then it would be a simple matter to convince the man to explain that the church had overreacted by grabbing him and that they apologized for any insult. He nodded to himself. Yes, that would be the way. Rufious would get what he needed without difficulty.

At last the door opened and the squad of four knights entered with a hooded man in their arms. With a silent gesture he indicated they should set him on the rack that filled the center of the room.

When they tried to strap him down Rufious waved them off. "No need for that. You can remove his hood and leave us alone."

The lead knight did as he bid and the squad hurried away.

The prisoner blinked and looked around as if uncertain where he'd ended up and why. Perfectly understandable reaction given the circumstances.

Rufious studied his guest with a frown. He'd expected someone far older to be serving the emperor directly. He doubted this fellow could be a day over twenty-five. Staring at the man wouldn't do him any good. Time to get underway.

"Do you know why you're here?" Rufious asked.

The young man shifted to look at him. "Because your White Knights kidnapped me?"

"Technically correct, but incomplete. The Forbidden Section is forbidden for a reason. It contains dangerous and corrupting knowledge. We can't let just anyone read it, even if he has the emperor's permission."

The young man smiled without humor before touching his head as if in pain. "I'll be certain to explain that to His Imperial Majesty when I return to the palace. I'm sure he'll appreciate the clarification about the limits to his authority."

Rufious's frown deepened. Clearly his guest didn't appreciate the danger of his current situation. "What's your name, boy?"

"Joran Den Cade."

He knew that name. He'd gained some prominence recently, but why?

Oh no.

The announcement the emperor sent out said his daughter was marrying Joran Den Cade, the hero of Stello Province. The man that had defeated a giant serpent and then negotiated a peace treaty with the native population. He might be the worst possible person for Rufious to have ordered brought in for questioning.

Time to try a different tactic. "Joran. May I call you Joran?"

"I believe Lord Den Cade would be proper, Your Grace. This is a formal inquisition, is it not?" Again the young man touched his temple and winced.

Had those idiots injured him even after Rufious's warning?

"Are you well, Lord Den Cade?"

"No. Your thugs separated me from my soulmate. My head feels like it's about to burst and my temper isn't much better. Worst of all, keeping a coherent thought in my head makes both of them even worse. If you have questions, ask them. Since I'm not strapped to this charming torture device, I assume you intend to release me at some point. Sooner would be better than later."

No wonder the young man wasn't properly intimidated. Not only was he the emperor's future son-in-law, but he'd lost contact with his soulmate. Since he'd broken no law or church custom, Rufious had little to threaten a man in his position with and this Den Cade boy knew it. He'd hoped to grab some high-ranking scribe, not a future member of the imperial family.

"Let's start with the basics: what did the emperor wish you to learn in the Forbidden Section?"

"I sought the origin of the serpent that appeared in Stello Province. I found clues that indicate there may be more of them. A man calling himself Samaritan is seeking to use the creatures to destroy the empire. Our hope was to figure out where the other creatures slept and secure them before Samaritan could wake them."

"And did you?"

"Not in the half hour I had to look before you brought me here."

Rufious winced. Perhaps he should have been more patient. Right now, it looked like the church sought to hinder the search for a threat to the entire empire. Given Samaritan's true identity, it might even look like they were siding with the former White Knight.

"Perhaps I acted too rashly. If only the emperor had reached out to us, this might have all been avoided."

Joran shrugged, his face twisting in a pained grimace. "I doubt His Imperial Majesty is used to having to reach out before issuing an order. Would you like me to mention your suggestion when next I speak with him?"

"That will not be—"

A heavy blow rattled the door. Who would dare interrupt him here?

Rufious strode over, ready to vent his frustration on whatever unlucky soul had sought him out. He unlocked the door and slammed it open. The leader of the White Knight squad he'd sent to capture Joran waited outside.

"Were my orders unclear?" Rufious asked.

"No, Your Grace. But an important development has occurred."

"Fine. What is it?"

"The First Legion is marching on the church with the Iron Princess at its head. Her Majesty does not look pleased."

"My fiancée is doubtless wondering why the church felt the need to kidnap me while I carried out her father's orders. I recommend explaining quickly, as she's not known for her patience."

Rufious ground his teeth. How much worse could this situation get?

He grabbed Joran by the sleeve and dragged him out into the hall. "The church thanks you for your cooperation. You're free to go."

"Thank you. If someone would be kind enough to direct me

to the exit nearest the approaching legion, I'll do my best to convince Alexandra not to burn your church down."

Rufious nearly choked. "She wouldn't dare."

"Have you met Alexandra? I'm sure burning down the First Church to The One God would cause all sorts of problems, but if you think that would stop her when she's on the warpath, you really don't know her at all. Don't worry, once she sees I'm okay, I'm sure she'll do the right thing."

Rufious just pointed down the hall. "Show him out."

When both men had gone, he held his head in his hands. Septimus was going to be furious when he found out what happened. And Rufious didn't even want to think about the emperor's reaction when Joran told him everything he said.

If by the end of the day Rufious remained a cardinal, he'd consider himself fortunate indeed. Mainly because it meant he still had a head attached to his neck.

———

Mia felt like a mushroom growing out of a rotten log as she rode along beside Alexandra at the head of the First Legion. She'd been surprised both by the speed with which the legion deployed and that the emperor had allowed it. Mia hadn't even been in the room when Alexandra told him what happened to Joran, but she'd heard his furious shout clearly enough. Somehow Mia doubted he cared about Joran as much as he did anyone having nerve enough to trouble someone acting on his direct orders. Whatever the case, having the entire First Legion march up to the church should be enough to get Joran released.

At least she hoped it did. Given Alexandra's mood, anything less than full and rapid compliance would lead to trouble.

As they approached the main entrance, a familiar tingle ran through Mia's body. Like lightning crackling through her veins, her strength flooded back. And with it came her awareness of Joran. They hadn't hurt him, thank The One God.

"He's coming, Majesty," Mia said.

As if summoned by her words, the front door opened and Joran emerged beside a White Knight. The knight had his arm in a firm grip.

Fury not dissimilar to what she'd felt when the dagger pierced his arm filled her. How dare anyone manhandle her soulmate!

Mia dismounted and sprinted up the stairs. She wrapped Joran in a hug. "Are you okay?"

"Yes, my captors were surprisingly gentle. It must have taken a great deal out of you. I'm sorry."

Mia nearly cried. He'd been kidnapped and questioned by the Inquisition and Joran's first thought was concern for her.

"I'm fine now. Is this asshole one of the ones that kidnapped you?"

"Yes."

Before he could flinch, Mia punched the White Knight right between the eyes. With her enhanced strength behind the blow, the unlucky man fell like a sledgehammered steer.

"I've been wanting to do that since they grabbed you."

Joran grinned. "I know, I can feel your satisfaction. I never doubted you'd come for me."

"Thank Alexandra too. I've never seen her so angry. The emperor wasn't exactly thrilled either."

"I imagine not." Joran took her hand and for the first time since they took him, Mia knew everything would be okay.

They walked back to the legion. Alexandra had dismounted and as soon as they arrived, jumped into Joran's arms. She kissed him and Mia felt a shared tingle. Talk about a sweet reward.

"Are you hurt?" Alexandra asked when she finally released her death grip.

"No. They were remarkably gentle given the Inquisition's reputation. I think the cardinal I spoke with wanted to scare me into telling them why the emperor sent me to the Forbidden Section. I gave him a tiny taste of the truth, but not all of it. I don't think they had any idea who they'd grabbed."

"Father doesn't actually want me to do anything drastic, so we'd better head back to the palace."

"I do have one request, if it's possible."

"As long as you don't want me to commit an atrocity, consider it possible."

"In that case, I'd like to swing by the library and collect the contents of the Forbidden Section. I think I'd prefer to continue my research in the safety of the palace."

Alexandra grinned. "That's a great idea. Let's see if they dare complain."

Marching several thousand heavily armed soldiers into the plaza in front of the library did wonders to eliminate complaints. Joran, Alexandra, Mia, and a full century of soldiers strode into the library, bypassed the front desk, and made straight for the empty hall that led to the Forbidden Section.

When they arrived, the door remained open and the books she'd tossed aside in her feverish attempt to access the secret door still lay on the floor where she'd left them.

Joran glanced at her. "What happened?"

She winced. "I may have gotten carried away. I hope I didn't damage any of them."

"I'm sure the information remains intact and that's what

matters. Let's gather everything and get out of here. I've lost some of my love for the library today."

For her part, Mia now despised the library with a burning passion. If she never set foot in the building again, it would suit her perfectly fine.

Half the soldiers got to work gathering up books while the rest kept watch with narrow, suspicious eyes. Mia suspected that if she saw her own eyes, they'd look exactly the same. She didn't plan to relax until they'd returned safely to the palace.

"Joran?"

She went for her sword only to spot the timid, blond provincial peeking between a pair of soldiers.

Joran laid a hand on her shoulder. "No need to give Julian a heart attack."

He went out into the hall and Mia followed, determined not to let him get more than an arm's length away from her.

"Sorry about the chaos," Joran said. "We've decided to complete our studies at the palace."

"You're... You're not really supposed to take any books out of the library."

Joran smiled, the kind one, not the mean one. "Special circumstances, my friend. Should anyone object, these fine gentlemen behind me stand ready to answer all complaints. You'll find the men of the First Legion highly competent at dealing with that sort of thing."

Her enhanced hearing brought Julian's gulp through loud and clear. A perfectly natural response from a civilian confronted by a century of legionnaires.

Alexandra emerged from the room. "We've got everything. Let's head back. No need to antagonize the church any more than necessary."

"If anyone gives you grief," Joran said. "Get a message to me at the palace. I'm sure I can find a position for you as my assistant or something."

Julian's eyes widened. "You think they might dismiss me because we're friends?"

"I doubt it, but then again, I have no idea how vindictive the church might be. If they can't hurt me directly, hurting my friend might be the next best option. Either way, you know I'll be there if you need me."

Joran and Julian shook hands before he and Mia fell in behind the legionnaires.

"That was very kind of you," Mia said.

"It was the least I could do. I hate the idea of my friends suffering because of my choices."

"None of this is your fault."

"Maybe not, but I still feel like we've stepped into a hornet's nest. Things may get way worse before they get better."

Mia tried to think of something worse than getting separated from Joran and failed. Whatever did end up happening, she'd be ready.

CHAPTER 5

Samaritan stood in front of a piece of polished steel that served him as a mirror and focused on the ether. The scars he'd gained from his near death at the hands of the church's hunters wavered and vanished as the illusion settled over them. He memorized the shape of the ether and released the spell. Restoring the illusion would be simple enough, far simpler than maintaining it for the entire trip to Dwarfhome, the provincial capital.

After considerable arguing, he'd convinced the rebels to guide him to the dwarven city. They thought him mad and repeatedly pointed out that access to the governor's residence was heavily restricted. He assured them that he had a way in and to let him worry about it.

Along the way, they also planned to investigate the two lava pools Grub mentioned on the off chance one of them had the warning markers indicating one of the giant beasts rested inside. He held little hope that something so important would lie along well-known paths, but if he didn't take the time to check, he'd feel awfully stupid if he was wrong.

He collected his satchel and winced at how light it felt. The rebels had no access to alchemy supplies and his personal stockpile in the ruins had nearly run out just before he left to explore Stello Province. Having to depend on only his meager magical talents to back up his sword skills left him a bit nervous.

Of course, if he ended up having to fight his way out of trouble, then something had gone terribly wrong.

As prepared as possible, Samaritan stepped out into the tunnel and made the short walk to the central gathering area. A dozen dwarves lounged around drinking the brew they fermented from mushroom juice. He'd tried a sip last night and nearly vomited. During his many travels both within and beyond the empire, he'd drunk and eaten some truly horrid things, but mushroom liquor took the prize for worst thing to date.

As far as he could tell, the rebels seemed more interested in getting drunk and lounging around than fighting the current government. Perhaps in dwarf culture being lazy made you a rebel. Based on everything he'd read and the few dwarves he'd met in Tiber, industriousness seemed bred into the people. Of course, there were exceptions to every rule.

Grub set his mug down and picked up a bundle of cloth before coming to join Samaritan. "This is the best we had."

Samaritan took the bundle and shook it out. The dark-brown cloak would barely reach his knees, but it should serve as a replacement for his signature white cloak while he visited Dwarfhome. "This is fine, thank you. Are you ready to leave?"

"Pretty near. Two of the others are preparing packs. They'll only give us what they can spare, so we may have to forage. The hunting isn't bad in the wild areas, assuming you're not fussy."

Samaritan snorted. He cared for food only insomuch as it kept him moving forward on his quest for revenge. If it tasted good, so much the better. He'd been surprised at how tasty some of the lizardmen's food had been.

A pair of unenthusiastic dwarves stomped toward them, each carrying a leather pack. The one on the left also had a sheathed shortsword in his off hand. Samaritan found he had trouble judging how old they were. Likely even the youngest were decades older than him.

He shook away the random, pointless thought and accepted a pack. It had decent heft. Perhaps they'd been more generous than he expected.

Grub shrugged into his pack and belted the shortsword at his waist. "This way."

He marched to the far end of the central cave and down a tunnel Samaritan had yet to explore. In fact he had yet to explore anything beyond the tunnel they followed down from the surface and the small area around his room and the meeting area.

At the mouth of the tunnel Grub stopped. "You need a light?"

Of course. Dwarves, like the lizardmen, had darkvision. Lucky for Samaritan, he knew that spell. "No, thank you."

He concentrated and drew two tiny threads of ether through his eyes and willed the darkvision spell to activate. The blackness beyond the cavern turned to gray and slightly blurry details emerged. Though far from ideal, it would keep him from running into the walls or other obstacles.

Grub set out at a steady plod. With his longer legs Samaritan had no trouble keeping up. The two companions stuck to the main tunnel for what felt like hours in the silent darkness.

They made good progress. At least it felt like good progress to Samaritan who had no real idea how far they had to go or how long it would take to reach the city.

About the time his stomach started growling Grub stopped and cocked his head. "There's a vein of bright crystal up ahead. We can take a lunch break."

Samaritan's pleasure at hearing a voice, even the voice of his less-than-enthusiastic guide, surprised him. Perhaps the darkness pressed down on him more than he realized. If he had to live down here, he'd certainly be as eager to partake in the mushroom liquor as the dwarves.

"How do you know?"

"Look at the rock through the ether and you'll see a thin golden vein. That always connects to bright crystal."

Samaritan looked closely and thought he saw a line as fine as spider silk that glowed golden in the ether, but it might just as well have been his imagination producing what Grub described. "You're a wizard? I didn't know the dwarves had a magical tradition."

"Not surprised. Geomancers were never common and since we joined the empire, anyone with the gift is discouraged from mentioning it, or, the stones forbid, showing what they can do. The last thing anyone wants for their children is to draw the church's attention. The priests would claim the young one had been possessed by an earth demon or something equally stupid."

"I regret to admit that's exactly what would happen." They rounded a corner and off to one side of the main tunnel found a small chamber filled with glowing golden crystals. "Beautiful. Did your people make these chambers?"

"No." Grub took off his pack and settled on the hard stone

floor. "The ether causes them to form naturally and, as far as anyone can tell, randomly."

Samaritan sat across from his suddenly chatty guide and released the darkvision spell. He blinked and blew out a breath. Even that tiny flow of ether slowly wore him out. Without the spell active, the crystals appeared even more stunning, like see-through gold. He'd never seen anything like it and allowed himself a moment to savor the view.

She would've loved this.

The old pain came crashing in, obliterating any pleasure he felt. His soulmate would never see anything again thanks to the empire. He couldn't forget that, not even for a moment.

Refocusing on his mission, Samaritan took out a preserved piece of mystery meat and bit into it. Salty and bland, probably the best he dared hope for given what they likely had to hunt down here.

Determined to learn all he could about his momentary allies he asked, "You mentioned the ether. Where did you learn that name? In the south, the locals believed what their shamans saw were spirits. I've only heard The One True God cultists use that phrase."

"The archbishop taught it to me," Grub said. "For a long time, geomancers thought we worked with the will of the stone. Not so different from spirits I guess. What she described sounded much more sensible."

Samaritan nodded. Everything he'd read in his broken redoubt suggested that the ones that built it had a much deeper and more robust understanding of magic. Certainly their ideas made more sense than vague, spiritual platitudes. At least they appealed to him and his dead faith.

"So are you a cultist or a rebel?"

Grub shrugged and swallowed. "Both, I guess. The cult's promises to teach me more about how the magic works excites me in a way I haven't felt since I first learned about magic. On the other hand, I do want to see the empire and their sympathizers kicked out of Dwarfhome. Or failing that their bodies carried out. I'm not fussy as long as they're gone."

Samaritan smiled inwardly. Grub's bitterness nearly matched his own. Somehow that made him feel like he could trust the dwarf more than he'd originally feared.

"How long will it take us to reach the lava pits?"

Grub stuffed his pouch of jerky back in his pack. "The first pit is about twenty miles from here. Barring trouble, we should arrive sometime tomorrow. The second one is about halfway between our base and Dwarfhome. Probably a week's walk from the first pit. What are we looking for exactly? Maybe I can help you search."

Since Grub knew how to view the ether, it might be worthwhile to explain. "Assuming the beast I'm seeking is sealed away the same as the serpent, you need to find a glowing symbol that looks like the monster in question surrounded by a circle. The ancient empire meant these ethereal brands to be warnings, but they also serve as markers."

"Assuming you don't care what you unleash," Grub said.

"As long as it kills imperials, I don't."

Sweat ran down Samaritan's face and plastered his tunic to his back. A dull, red glow appeared just ahead at the end of a side tunnel Grub had led them down about an hour ago. A full day had passed since they set out on their journey, though how Grub could tell that Samaritan had no idea. They'd stopped to sleep once, though Samaritan mostly struggled to get comfortable on the smooth patch of stone while Grub snored contentedly as though resting on the softest feather mattress.

Shaking his head, Samaritan focused on the stone around them. No sign of a mark and he'd seen nothing on the way in either. Such a wide-open access indicated that they'd chosen the wrong pit. The last one had been sealed behind yards of solid stone. This was just too easy.

Twenty paces from the end of the tunnel Samaritan had to stop. The heat seared his lungs and made it nearly impossible to breathe. "Let's go back. This can't be the place."

"Wait there. I'll make sure." Ether swirled around Grub and the dwarf pushed through the heat to the end of the tunnel. A moment later he returned and shook his head. "Just lava, no beast."

They hurried back until the temperature reached a tolerable level. Samaritan slumped, his back pressed against the relatively cool stone of the tunnel wall. He sucked in deep lungfuls of air. The lava must have been closer here. In the southern mountain, the heat hadn't been nearly this bad.

"I always forget how fragile you humans are. A little extra heat and you go all to pieces."

Samaritan looked up at him. "You did something with the ether to protect yourself at the end. I've never seen that spell before."

"I'm not surprised. It's a geomancer spell called Lava Walker. It protects you from intense heat. Some of the old timers say the great masters could actually use it to walk over lava, though no one living has that sort of power. I can only maintain it for about ten seconds."

"Sounds useful." Samaritan pushed himself up. "Let's get moving."

He'd only taken a single step before a tremor ran through the tunnel. Being underground during an earthquake would not be ideal.

"What was that?" he asked.

Grub shook his head. "Not sure. Not a quake, I'd see it rattling the ether. Oh, no."

Samaritan turned slowly to watch a creature—he wasn't sure what else to call it—with four legs, the head of a lion, and the tail of a scorpion all made of lava stalk down the tunnel. An aura of black, twisted ether surrounded the thing. Not corruption like the serpent or Black Bile, but something equally horrible. Something demonic.

"Do we run or will that trigger an attack?"

"It's a lava ghost. They don't hunt for meat, but for the pleasure of killing. The vile things are rare. I mean really rare. What in the world caused it to show up here?"

"Who cares?" Samaritan asked. "Unless you know how to kill it, we need to get the hell out of here."

"No, we can't outrun it. We need to hide. Press your back flat against the wall and don't make a sound."

That sounded insane, but in this place, ignoring Grub made even less sense. Steeling himself, Samaritan pressed his back flat to the tunnel wall and Grub joined him a moment later. Ether swirled around them. Yet another spell Samaritan didn't recognize formed around them.

The lava ghost stopped and swung its head around, clearly confused. It bared its fangs and lava dripped on the floor, creating sizzling puddles.

Samaritan held his breath as it drew closer.

The creature stared right at him without seeming to see anything.

Samaritan feared it might hear his pounding heart.

Instead, the lava ghost loosed a frustrated roar, spun, and stalked off the way it had come. Hopefully it would swim away and trouble some other unlucky soul.

A minute passed, then another and still no word from Grub about moving on. Samaritan dared a glance at his companion and found his gaze fixed dead ahead seemingly unconscious.

He quickly pressed a hand to the dwarf's neck. Thank goodness he found a pulse.

He snapped his fingers in front of Grub's nose but drew no reaction. The spell shielding them appeared to still be in place. That had to be a horrible strain on him.

Grub must have entered some sort of trance to help keep the spell functional. Probably the only way to bring him out of it would be to break the spell. No easy task given Samaritan's limited magical ability. On the other hand, continuing on without his guide would be suicide.

Besides, he felt a certain kinship with the dwarf. Something he hadn't felt with anyone in a long time. Drawing ether to him until he reached his limit, he formed it into a hammer and swung it at the wall Grub had made.

The spell shattered into glittering motes.

Grub blew out a long breath. "I knew you'd figure it out."

So saying the dwarf fell to the tunnel floor, completely insensible.

Samaritan glowered at his unconscious companion. "I suppose now I'll have to carry you out of here."

A single attempt to lift Grub convinced Samaritan that dragging the dwarf would be his best bet. Despite his diminutive stature, Grub felt like he weighed a good two hundred pounds. How he weighed so much Samaritan neither knew nor cared. No doubt some quirk of the dwarven constitution.

By the time they made it back to the nearest bright crystal cave, Samaritan's entire body felt limp. He slumped against the wall and closed his eyes. Utter exhaustion claimed him.

CHAPTER 6

Septimus Salonius, better known as His Holiness the Pope, held his head in his hands as he listened to his normally reliable aide Cardinal Rufious. The two men were alone in Septimus's far-too-modest office. On a stand off to one side hung his itchy robe and giant hat of office. He wanted to ask one of the historians why they had such a ridiculous outfit for the most powerful man in the empire, but he figured that was the sort of thing they'd expect him to know already so he kept his questions to himself.

"Are you listening, Holiness?" Rufious asked.

"Unfortunately, I heard every word. Of all the people you might have grabbed, why in The One God's name did you choose the princess's fiancé?"

"As I said, I didn't know who he was until after I grabbed him. I wasn't invited to the announcement and so had no idea what the man looked like. It's just rotten luck really. Now the head librarian says the First Legion took every book in the Forbidden Section. I grant you that we keep the really damning stuff here, but if a competent researcher goes through everything there…"

"Yes, I get the idea. I suppose I'll have to go talk to Marcus and register my displeasure at his behavior."

"Actually…"

Septimus shot him a hard look. He knew that tone. Rufious was about to suggest something he didn't want to hear. "Actually what?"

"I think this might be an opportunity to bring the royal family in on our secret."

"Which one? We have so many secrets I can't even keep track of them all."

"The big one."

"Are you mad? You want me to admit to the emperor that the entire church is built on the lie that The One God is real and the Prophet was actually a prophet and not a raving lunatic slash genius alchemist? If we share that secret, the church is done."

"No, it isn't. The empire can't afford for the church to be done. The faith serves as a unifying force among the disparate peoples. It's basically the only thing everyone pretty much agrees on. And the emperor needs everyone to agree on it. Marcus might hate it, but you will find no more powerful or enthusiastic supporter than him."

"He'll also have a sword hanging over our head for however long the empire lasts."

"A sword he won't dare drop. Especially now, with all the other threats facing the empire. If the church and throne work together, we'll all have a better chance of surviving. Believe me, Septimus, when I tell you the people beyond the empire's borders will look no more favorably on churchmen than they will imperials, legionnaires, and nobles."

Septimus's brow creased even as his headache pounded all the harder. Rufious had a point, damn him. Admitting the church's biggest secret would also make a convenient way to cover their overeagerness to find out what Marcus's agent intended.

"I'll consider it. Have we received an imperial summons yet?"

"No, but it's only a matter of time."

"You'll come with me and offer an apology to the noble boy." Rufious opened his mouth but Septimus cut him off. "No excuses. If the pope has to humble himself then so does a cardinal. When this meeting is over, the church and throne will either be welded together as never before or there will be a split like nothing the empire has ever seen. The worst thing is, I can't decide which is most likely."

"The worst thing," Rufious said. "Is that the answer is out of our control."

Septimus thumped his head on the desk. Why did Rufious never say something to make things better? And why did he have to be right?

———

Joran blinked sleep from his eyes and tried his best to focus. He and Mia had joined the imperial family—the immediate family, he had yet to meet Marcus's wife and children—in the same salon where Alexandra had gotten her dressing down for assuming command of the Second Legion. The atmosphere felt tense again for this meeting, but the tension had a different edge. Like they were all united against an outside enemy, in this case the church.

In the two days since Alexandra and Mia freed him from

the church, he'd managed about six hours of sleep as he tried to get the many books they collected in some sort of order. He hadn't even begun to actually study them. Still, he'd made some progress in the form of the scroll he held in his right hand.

Alexandra looked beautiful as always in a robe colored Cade Cerulean. She left her father's side to hug him when they stopped. "You look tired. You've hardly visited the suite since we got back."

"Too much to do. I appreciate your concern." He kissed her cheek.

"Well, my boy," the emperor said from his crimson chair. He wore a relaxed smile today instead of the angry frown last time they visited here. "Have you figured out what the church is up to?"

"Not yet, but I can tell you they're still hiding something."

The emperor chuckled. "I'm sure, but what do you think they're hiding in particular?"

"That I'm less certain of. All I know for sure is when I went through the books we took, there are gaps. My theory is that the church has hidden a number of the most dangerous volumes somewhere else. The church basement being my guess." Joran held up the scroll. "This details the gaps. How we can convince someone to turn over the missing tomes is beyond me."

"So Septimus is playing games." The emperor's tone sent a chill up Joran's spine. "I can make turning over the missing documents a requirement for returning to my good graces. It would be helpful if you could provide me with some more details about what he's hiding."

Joran debated for a moment, but if there was ever a moment to reveal what he'd learned from Samaritan's note-book, this was it. "Whether the church is aware of it or not, I've come across some information that indicated alchemy isn't as special as we've been taught. It's simply another way of manipulating an energy field called the ether that is the source of all the magic used by our enemies."

Everyone stared at him, their mouths partway open. Mia only pretended shock of course. He'd already shared all this with her. The imperial family's reaction, on the other hand, appeared genuine.

When he could finally speak the emperor said, "That directly contradicts everything the Prophet taught us. Alchemy is supposed to be the purest skill handed down from The One God himself. Are you certain that's accurate?"

"I'm not certain about anything, but that is the most startling thing I've learned so far. If you wanted something to use when you speak to the pope, that struck me as the most likely to draw a reaction. I recommend drinking a detect-deception potion beforehand, so you can tell if his excuses are true or yet more lies."

"If it is true and the secret got out…" Marcus didn't have to finish the sentence.

They all knew what would happen. Faith in the church and its teachings would be called into question and given how closely people associated the empire and the church, it might make them question the emperor as well.

"All the stories we're told about the enemy being demon worshippers whose magic came from hell." Alexandra shook her head. "If we're all drawing from the same pool, it makes us no better than them."

"Not a word of this leaves this room." The emperor looked each of them in the eye ending with Joran. "I plan to summon Septimus for a meeting in one week. I want you to get as much information as possible and prepare some questions for me, especially regarding what you think they're hiding. We'll never have the bastard in a weaker position and I mean to make the most of it."

Joran nodded. He'd expected nothing less. Looked like more long nights in his future.

CHAPTER 7

Joran jotted another note on his list of questions for the emperor. For three days he'd been holed up in his new lab reading. Stacks of books from the Forbidden Section surrounded his desk. Even working twenty hours a day, he'd still only put a tiny dent in the pile. They'd all agreed that an assistant would be a bad idea given the sensitive nature of the information. Much as he would have liked the help, Joran didn't disagree with the decision.

And he had progressed. Despite the gaps, he made some fascinating discoveries, including some about the ether and the Black Iron Empire. One thing he found most interesting was that the empire's wizards didn't call the power they wielded "the ether." They simply called it magic. In fact, in everything he'd read, only Samaritan's journal used the phrase, "the ether." Where in the world had he picked that name up?

Joran grabbed the next book on his table and opened it. The black leather cover appeared well cared for without cracks or splits. He'd read two others like it, all from the Black Iron Empire. That empire had fallen about seven hundred years ago, which meant the books were older than that. Clearly some sort of preservative magic had been applied. He knew an alchemical oil that acted the same way, but that left a specific smell these books lacked.

Halfway down the page his eyes widened. It described a series of mental techniques that, properly applied, would allow someone with the necessary potential to see magic. Which meant to see the ether. That was the first step in becoming a wizard.

He'd barely read the next sentence when Mia entered bearing a tray loaded with food. How long since he'd eaten? Joran didn't remember. When he got involved with a project he often forgot to eat. It had been that way for years. Lucky for him, Mia brought something at regular intervals. She said keeping him fed beat having to help with the reading.

A safe distance from the books, they'd placed a small, portable desk for meals. She set the tray on it and he got his first look at the goodies. Ham-and-cheese sandwiches, wine, fruit, and nuts. Not bad at all.

"Thanks." Joran grabbed a sandwich and took a bite.

Mia smiled and sat across from him. "I can tell when you're hungry even if you can't. Anything interesting?"

"It's all interesting, but I found a book on how the Black Iron Empire trained its wizards, at least the first step. After we eat, I'm going to try and follow it. If I succeed, it will prove that I have wizard potential. I'm still a little vague on exactly what that means beyond the obvious. From what I can tell, no one can become a wizard without it, though there are apparently other paths to controlling magic."

"Like alchemy?" she asked.

"Exactly, though I've yet to see a mention of it in any of the books I've read. I'm starting to think that even if The One God didn't hand the knowledge directly down to him, the man we think of as the Prophet may well have been the source for the school of magic we call alchemy. The truth of how he actually came by the knowledge is another matter altogether. One I have yet to answer."

"Does it even matter how he came by the information to start with?"

"Not on a practical level, but if we knew the origin, we might be able to learn secrets the Prophet missed." Joran finished his meal and stood. "That hit the spot, thank you. How's Alexandra doing? We haven't had a war in a while, I imagine she's getting bored."

"If so, she's said nothing to me. Not that she says a great deal to me in any case. Are you sure you should be doing experiments now and not focusing on reading?"

Joran shrugged. She had a point, but now that he knew how to check and see if he had the potential to be a wizard, how could he not take the time to find out for sure?

"I'll leave you to it. Don't do anything crazy."

"I fear the ship has sailed on that one, but I will be careful."

"I'll take it." She gathered up the tray and took her leave before he had a chance to ask her to read anything. Joran didn't know exactly where she went, but their link never wavered. She probably kept watch on the lab from up the hall.

Shifting Mia's presence to the back of his mind, Joran returned to the workbench.

Now, let's see. He read a couple of pages and frowned.

Making the mental shift sounded simple enough, yet it said many wizards needed weeks or months of practice to manage it. Perhaps none of them had found their soulmate. The increased mental clarity should make this easy, assuming he actually had the potential.

Joran took a deep breath and let his vision defocus so the lab became blurry. Now he needed to imagine the real world as just an illusion lying over something greater. Picture reality parting like the curtains at the start of a play and see the ether beyond it.

He picked a spot in the wall and imagined it opening like a secret door.

When he did, swirling, chaotic light filled his vision. Colors he never imagined flashed and exploded around him.

"By The One God." How did the wizards ever make sense of this? It looked like pure chaos brought to life.

He closed his eyes and let the mental picture go. When he opened them again, the lab appeared normal again.

Turning back to the book he read some more. Now that he'd seen the ether, the book said he needed to present himself to the wizard's academy for proper training. Since that doubtless hadn't existed for nearly a thousand years, he'd have to hope for some other path to learning to wield the magic. Given the knowledge at his fingertips, it seemed impossible that he'd find nothing.

Joran grinned. He could be a wizard. A few days ago, he wouldn't have believed such a thing was possible. And if it was, he would have assumed he'd need to sell his soul to a demon to gain the power. While he still didn't know what it would take to draw on the magic, he at least knew he had the potential to use it.

How many others in the empire had that same potential? Quite a few, he guessed, but more importantly, should they be encouraged or should they remain in ignorance of their true potential?

He didn't know and figured the question should be answered by those far wiser than him.

———

Fane settled into her comfortable leather chair and considered the most recent message from her agent among the dwarves. Grub and Samaritan were supposed to be approaching the first lava pit soon. In fact, they may have reached it already. With any luck they'd find the second beast and more importantly some clue to the location of the Black Iron Empire's capital. She'd been searching for so long. All the lore she needed had to be there.

Samaritan claimed he found no clues about the capital's location in the serpent's lair, but she'd begun to suspect he was keeping secrets from her.

Her lips curled into a smile. Of course he kept secrets from her, just as she kept secrets from him. He wanted to unleash the hidden power and destroy the Tiberian Empire. Fane doubted he even knew that he sought a dragon, though given the monsters he'd found so far, another giant creature wouldn't come as a surprise.

She wanted it unleashed as well, but for a different reason. If she was right, setting the dragon free to wreak havoc on the world would also put it to sleep for centuries at least. If she knew where it slept, she could tap its power and increase her own or use it to create more-powerful servants. Unlike Samaritan, the chaos and destruction would be her means, not her end.

Still, perhaps learning a little bit more about her partner of convenience wouldn't be a bad idea. The White Knight Beastmaster captured probably knew plenty of secrets about Samaritan. She'd have to leave him alive for now for future interrogation. Assuming the mutated beasts hadn't devoured him already.

Closing her eyes Fane willed her mind across space until she found Beastmaster's crystal ball. For all his considerable skill in flesh shaping, he still lacked the ability to communicate over long distances without a focusing artifact.

It took less than a minute for the ageless youth to complete the connection. "I didn't expect to hear from you again so soon."

"Is the White Knight still alive?"

"For now. He's sneaky. So far, he's evaded my bigger pets and fled the small ones. I've been trying to think the best way to deal with him. Why?"

"Can you capture him alive?"

Though she didn't really perceive his physical form, Fane imagined his head cocked in confusion at her question. "He is captured. No one can get out of the maze. I can keep him alive easily enough. All I need to do is tell my pets not to kill him. There's plenty of fresh water and rats for him to hunt."

"Good, do that. I may want to speak with him at some point."

"Okay. How long do you want me to keep him?"

"Until I tell you otherwise."

"Sure, no need to be so crabby. Anything else?"

"No." She ended the spell and smiled. No one else dared call her crabby. Beastmaster was no fool, but he didn't fear her either. Plenty of people, all of them dead, would have said that made him a fool by definition, but Fane figured his personality just worked that way. He seemed to fear nothing and she sensed no deception when they spoke.

She shrugged and dismissed him from her thoughts. As long as he did good work and remained loyal, Beastmaster would have nothing to fear. If that changed, well, then they'd see. While she had no desire to fight him, it would be an interesting contest given how diametrically opposed their powers were.

A faint tingle in the back of her mind ended her speculation. She recognized the touch of her mist wraith's psychic presence.

"Go ahead."

I have arrived at the edge of the empire and should reach the capital in a few days.

"Good. You encountered no resistance?"

I've stayed in mist form. No one even sensed my presence. I wished to confirm that your orders haven't changed.

"They haven't. Get the sword. I don't care what you need to do."

Understood.

Wraith's presence vanished. Fane eagerly awaited her servant's results. Though she'd created it long ago, this was the first time she'd really get a chance to see what it could do in the field.

Not that she imagined the imperials, with their crude understanding of alchemy, posed a real threat to her mist wraith.

CHAPTER 8

Samaritan slept twice while he waited for Grub to wake. He assumed that meant he'd spent two days sitting in the bright crystal cave. Fear and boredom did strange things to a man. Several times he imagined the lava ghost had returned, but both times he woke up from the nightmare none the worse for wear.

In fact, to his considerable surprise, neither beast nor monster had troubled them in their hiding place. He assumed some unseen aspect of the magic kept them away.

And a good thing too. No way would he have been able to fight off anything remotely as dangerous as the lava ghost on his own. Though even if Grub were awake and in top shape, that thing would have been too much for them.

He dug a strip of jerky out of his pack, but before he had a chance to take a bite Grub groaned and sat up. The dwarf peered around the cave before finally focusing on Samaritan. "What happened?"

"You fainted. Your spell hid us from the lava ghost, but then you went into some kind of trance and even after the creature had gone, you seemed unable to release the spell. I shattered the illusion and when I did you collapsed. I dragged you here and have been waiting ever since. Is all well?"

Grub nodded. "Well enough. The trance is a trick geomancers learn to maintain a spell longer than we otherwise could. Basically, you don't feel the effects of channeling too much ether. Unfortunately, as you saw, it also leaves you stuck in the spell. If there's no one to snap you out of it, well, geomancers have died trapped in their own spells."

"A dangerous technique. I'm surprised you risked it." Samaritan offered him a piece of meat and Grub eagerly accepted.

"Not as risky as fighting a lava ghost," he said around a mouthful of food. "Once I get a meal in me, we can head for the next lava crevice."

"Unless it's directly on the way to Dwarfhome, let's skip it. I prefer to do my research first. Had I known about lava ghosts, I wouldn't have even suggested searching the first one."

"It's only a day out of our way, but if that's your wish, I won't argue. Though you should know that creatures like the lava ghost are exceptionally rare. It was just bad luck that we ran into this one. Plenty of dwarves wander the tunnels their whole lives and never see one."

"Be that as it may, I'd still rather not risk it. I have a hunch and it might well be totally off base, but my suspicion is that the beast I seek may give off corrupt energy. If I'm right, that might draw dangerous, evil creatures to its vicinity."

Grub finished his meal and stood. "Is that what happened with the first one?"

"No, but there also appeared to be no evil, magical creatures living in the jungle. It did use its magic to trick a pair of locals into believing it was a spirit worthy of releasing. I fear the giant beasts are more intelligent than I first gave them credit for. Of course, it might also be some sort of animal instinct as well. In any case, I mean to do my research then we can go directly to its location. Hopefully avoiding any other nasty surprises in the process."

"It sounds so easy when you say it."

Samaritan pushed himself to his feet and snorted a laugh. "You may be certain nothing about this task will be easy. I can guarantee you little, but I can guarantee you that."

As they left the bright crystal cave behind Grub said, "I appreciate you saving me. Before we left, I had my doubts about your loyalty. Lucky for me I was wrong about you."

Samaritan nodded but didn't speak. In truth, without Grub, he would've been totally lost down here. Sometimes desperation looked a great deal like loyalty.

———

Wraith floated invisible and intangible about fifty feet from Tiber's outer wall. It sensed the many thousands of humans inside the city. Each of them gave off a slight glow in the ether. Some brighter, some duller, but all tasty. Not that Wraith needed to eat; it simply enjoyed the feeling of mortals dying. All of the undead in its mistress's service did. Though smarter than some of its brethren, Wraith shared all of their hungers.

Well, it didn't matter, not today at least. Wraith had a mission to complete and hungers or not, the mist wraith would do well not to delay completing the task at hand. As it had heard the odd human Beastmaster say on occasion, Mistress Fane had a habit of getting grumpy. And a grumpy mistress frightened even Wraith.

The mist wraith flew up and over the city, keeping its senses alert for the largest concentration of corruption. That would be the black iron sword. They had plenty of black iron artifacts in the ruin the group called home, yet she wanted this particular sword back in the worst way.

If Wraith hadn't believed its mistress incapable of sentimentality, it would have assumed the fact that her master left the sword with her before he returned to wherever they came from made them somehow more valuable. Impossible, of course. The weapons must have some other, hidden value a lesser being like Wraith couldn't perceive.

It didn't take long to find the sword. A black mass of corruption sat near the heart of the imperial palace. Wraith flew closer, confirming that it'd found what it sought.

Diving like a hunting hawk, Wraith passed through wall after wall, finally ending up in a sealed chamber. Glittering treasures filled niches and covered shelves. Ignoring the useless baubles, Wraith flew directly over to the black iron sword. It sat on a plain stone table. No warding magic glittered in the ether.

Of course it didn't. These primitive humans had no concept of magic. Amazing that they'd accomplished all they had without it.

Wraith took its physical form, that of a cloaked human concealed by darkness. It picked up the sword and swung the weapon a few times. Everything appeared as it should. Now the hard part—getting out of here with its mistress's prize.

Pity Wraith couldn't turn back into mist with the sword, but only its physical form dissolved; anything it held ended up on the ground. It found a smooth section of wall with a wheel built into it.

The door at last. Wraith had never seen one like this, but a door was a door.

A yank with its free hand didn't even rattle the door in its frame. Wrenching the wheel left then right produced equally poor results. Clearly the humans had a way to enter and exit this room. If they could do it, Wraith could as well. It just needed to know the secret.

Leaning the sword against the wall, Wraith turned intangible again and slipped through the door without issue. Outside waited a long, empty hall devoid of humans to question. Growing more annoyed by the second, Wraith flew on.

Ignoring both walls and doors, Wraith focused on the ether, or more specifically the little golden specks that represented humans. It found one soon enough, a female dressed in a white uniform. The tray she carried clattered to the ground when Wraith appeared before her.

She tried to run, but Wraith grabbed her by the neck and drained some of her life force. Her body trembled and for a moment it feared it had taken too much. Not that the mist wraith cared if it killed the human, but if it did so before she answered its questions, another would need to be found.

"Be still, human. Tell me how to open the locked door at the end of the empty hall and I will let you go." That Wraith would let her go directly to whatever fate awaited her soul it declined to mention.

"You can't," she said in a shaky voice. "That's the royal vault. Only members of the imperial family can open it."

If Wraith had had a jaw it would have clenched it in frustration. "Where can I find the imperial family?"

"The throne room. His Imperial Majesty is having an important meeting. All servants were ordered out of the area. It's directly above the vault."

"You've been most helpful, human." Wraith drove its claw into her heart, stopping it instantly. A relatively painless death and the best reward Wraith had to offer.

Leaving the corpse where it fell, Wraith returned to the vault and turned into a black mist with glowing eyes. This form always unnerved those who saw it. Not that they often lived long enough for Wraith to savor the emotions.

Time to see how an emperor reacted.

Wraith rose toward the ceiling. At the very least it should be interesting.

CHAPTER 9

Joran stood beside Alexandra, who stood beside her father's throne. Marcus stood on the other side and Mia hid behind the throne, armed and ready should any danger appear. The emperor himself dressed in crimson and gold robes with the eagle crown perched on his head. The usually busy throne room sat silent and empty today. No one else needed to know what would transpire here.

The doors opened with a dull thud and Pope Septimus Salonius entered along with the cardinal that kidnapped Joran. The pope wore his full regalia, including the ridiculous hat. In his right hand he gripped a white staff trimmed in gold. Looked like everyone had gone all out for the meeting. No surprise there. Joran doubted the two most powerful men in the empire met very often.

At the foot of the throne, the cardinal took a knee, but the pope looked Emperor Marcus dead in the eye, showing not the least deference. The staring match lasted just long enough to feel uncomfortable before the pope finally spoke.

"You summoned us."

"Indeed," the emperor said. "I wished to know why you felt assaulting a man acting under my writ was a good idea."

"*We* wished to know this man's purpose in visiting the Forbidden Section of the library. Had you sent us a note indicating your plans, it would have made things a good deal simpler for everyone."

Joran wanted to wince, but his training held. Alexandra reached out and took his hand, whether offering or seeking support he didn't know, but he appreciated the gesture either way.

"I don't answer to you." The emperor's voice cut the air, so sharp was his tone. "If I decide I need to know something, it's not for you to tell me otherwise. When I give an order, I expect it to be obeyed, regardless of whom I give it to."

Alexandra squeezed his hand, probably remembering their earlier conversation with her father about obedience.

"And I am the pope," Septimus said. "My duty is to guide the spiritual wellbeing of the empire. Those books hold information that might, in the wrong hands, corrupt the souls of the innocent. Knowing who and why that information is accessed is my responsibility."

The pope blew out a long breath. "That said, my aide did act somewhat abruptly. He joined me today to offer his most sincere apologies to the young man he inconvenienced. Go on, Rufious."

The cardinal stood and looked right at Joran. "My apologies, Lord Den Cade. Had I known your identity, I would have approached you in a far different way."

Much as Joran would have liked to rub the arrogant prick's nose in his mistake, there was a time for gloating and a time for magnanimity. This was clearly the latter.

"Not at all, Cardinal Rufious. I understand you have your

duty to fulfill just as I do. Hopefully we can avoid any other unpleasantness in the future."

Rufious offered a polite bow. "As you say, sir."

"Now that we've taken care of that business," the pope said. "Did you need anything else?"

"As long as you're here." The emperor's tone had moderated to something almost friendly. "We did have a few questions. Joran?"

A lump formed in Joran's throat. The emperor wanted him to question the pope? No one had mentioned that, at least not that he recalled, during the discussion they'd had just before the pope's arrival. Granted, he hadn't gotten enough sleep over the past week, but he assumed he'd have remembered that.

The pope turned his cold, dark gaze on Joran. He found nothing fatherly or comforting in that look. Still, the questions needed to be asked.

"Your Holiness, I appreciate your consideration. I suppose my first question is, would it be possible to gain access to the volumes you've stored outside the Forbidden Section?"

The pope gave away little, but the slight tightening around his eyes told Joran all he needed to know. His guess had been right.

"What volumes do you mean?" the pope asked.

"There are obvious gaps in a variety of collections. I've prepared a list if you'd like to read it. I can't get a complete understanding of the situation until those gaps are filled."

The pope said nothing, simply staring at Joran as if willing him to retract the question. Under other circumstances that gaze might have convinced him to do exactly that. Surrounded by the imperial family and with the emperor's backing, he felt he had a strong enough position to stand his ground. Not that he found that a comfortable feeling.

Cardinal Rufious leaned in and whispered something to him. The pope's face twisted in distaste, but he finally nodded.

"What I'm about to tell you is the darkest secret of the church. The secret we sought to protect from all those that wanted to reveal it."

"We're listening," the emperor said.

"The One God isn't real. The Prophet, for all his genius in alchemy, was also a madman. As best we could determine, he made The One God up from whole cloth. His name was Xing Lai and he came from the northeast, apparently fleeing some internal strife among his allies. The details are a little vague, but it seems your ancestor was keen enough to learn his secrets that he played along with his One God story. Later on, the first pope and the second emperor conspired to hide the truth. The church never forgot, but at some point, the imperial family did."

Silence filled the room. Joran had always harbored doubts. He suspected most of those whose faith came more as a matter of social norms rather than true belief did. But to hear it said out loud by the leader of the church was another matter altogether.

"And when it became clear that my ancestors had forgotten, it never occurred to you or one of the earlier popes to remind us?" Joran struggled not to show his relief when the emperor took over the conversation.

"Of course not," Septimus said. "Information is power. Having the imperial family believe that the church actually acted on behalf of a powerful, supernatural force increased ours. Rest assured this isn't something we share among the priesthood and lay followers. In fact, only the pope and his aide, that is Rufious and I, know the truth. When the time comes to choose a successor, we will pass the secret on."

"Why share it now?" the emperor asked.

"Because a threat has appeared. A threat to both the church and the empire. You know the man as Samaritan. Once he was known as Bellator, a most devout and loyal White Knight. Too devout as it turned out. He wanted to go on a quest to find where the Prophet came from. He felt called he said and no words, even mine, would dissuade him. So I sent a team of hunters to deal with him."

"Unsuccessfully it seems," the emperor said.

"Yes. They believed that they had killed Bellator and so did we, until he reappeared in Stello Province. Another team has set out to clean up the mess. If they succeed, great. If not, well, more help rather than less would be good. I think we both know that having a strong, healthy church is good for the empire. Given that, I've deemed telling you the truth to be the best course."

The emperor leaned back on his throne, a thoughtful look on his face. Joran would have liked to see his thoughts right then. His own raced a thousand miles an hour. The implications of the national religion being a lie were enormous. Millions of citizens prayed to The One God believing he heard them even if he didn't answer. Spreading that faith drove a huge part of the empire's foreign policy as well.

Joran gave a mental shake of his head. Lucky for him, he didn't have to decide this sort of thing.

At last, the emperor leaned forward again. "You're right. A strong church is in the empire's best interest and we will keep your secret. However, there can be no more secrets between us. Whatever books you've hidden will be brought to the palace for Joran to study. All of them. No excuses. Regular meetings will be necessary as well. Not between us. That would raise too many questions. Perhaps the cardinal and my son would be a good pair to handle it."

"Your terms are acceptable," Septimus said. "Rufious can work out the details of the meetings with the prince. As for the books, we'll need a day to gather and prepare them for transport. Some are quite delicate and will need to be carefully packed."

That set off huge alarm bells in Joran's mind. With its wealth, the church should have access to all the preserving oil they might ever want. The only reason they might need extra time was to sort out more of the collection.

He slipped past Alexandra and whispered that very thing in the emperor's ear.

"Joran has kindly offered to help with the packing and is willing to join you right now. "

The pope's face twisted in distaste. "How very kind."

A chill ran down Joran's spine that had nothing to do with the pope's current displeasure. He'd been practicing looking at the ether and had gotten to the point where he could do so without getting completely overwhelmed by the chaos.

He shifted his gaze and studied the entire throne room. Something dark swirled around the floor. He didn't recognize it, but doubted anything that looked like that could be good.

Joran leaned in and whispered to Alexandra. "What's directly below the throne room?"

"The royal vault. Why?"

"Something's happening down there. I can't tell what, but it looks bad."

"That's not possible. Only the imperial family can access that room and we're all here. Besides, this isn't the time to discuss it."

"Is something wrong?" the emperor asked.

"No, Father," Alexandra said. "Joran thought—"

Her explanation ended as a dark mist rose up out of the floor. Glowing red eyes formed in the black cloud and it glared around at the group.

"A demon," Septimus said in disbelief.

The darkness congealed into a cloaked humanoid figure. "Compliments will gain you nothing. I require the vault door opened. Comply or every one of you will die."

Mia darted out from behind the throne, sword raised, and charged.

An instant before her sword would have struck home, the creature turned back into mist.

Mia's sword passed through it, doing no damage.

She leapt back and the thing reformed.

"How rude. Just for that, I'm going to kill you first." It turned into the black mist again and then vanished altogether.

Nothing had the power to simply vanish. Joran shifted his view to the ether and sure enough spotted the dark shape. With all his concentration he focused on sharing his vision with Mia.

She stiffened and immediately leapt back, avoiding a ghostly claw by inches.

"We need to get out of here," Joran said. "Mia can't stop that thing and I doubt the guards can either."

"Where do we go to escape a demon?" Alexandra asked.

"The church," Septimus said. "There's a safe room in the basement. No evil can enter."

Joran only half heard what they were saying. Most of his focus remained on Mia as she played tag with the ghostly creature. Her speed kept her safe, but that thing appeared unharmed by imperial steel.

How did you even kill something made of air?

"Have you tested this safe room?" the emperor asked. "If you're counting on the power of a god that doesn't exist, I have my doubts about how safe we'll be."

"You think you're any better off here?" Septimus countered.

"Whatever we're going to do, we need to do it quickly," Joran said. "The monster looks like it's getting frustrated. If it gets sick of chasing Mia, we're next. And I can't share my sight with any of you."

"Fine," the emperor said. "We'll make a run for the church. Let's go."

He got up off the throne and they raced for the door.

Halfway there the darkness reformed into the cloaked figure. "You're not going anywhere. My mistress desires the return of her black iron sword. I refuse to return to her in disgrace. Give me the sword and you may all continue breathing for a little while longer."

"Maybe we should just give it to him," Marcus said.

"Finally, one of you shows some wisdom."

"No," the emperor said. "It'll just kill us when it has what it wants. We can't trust a demon to honor its word."

Mia skidded to a stop beside Joran. "Thanks. I don't know what I would have done if you hadn't let me see that thing."

Joran nodded, not taking his eyes off the demon lest he lose track of it. The lights of the ether had begun to give him a headache. In his brief experiments with his new sight, he found using it for too long tended to result in a pounding pain at his temples.

It made no move to attack, but it also didn't seem inclined to get out of their way. A standoff then and them without any weapons worth a damn.

"Any thoughts on how we might get past it?" he asked, keeping his voice pitched low.

"I can't hurt it or anything. It's like fighting air."

"Air, huh?" He hated to use alchemist's fire in the palace, but his options were limited. "Do you have a throwing dagger with you?"

"Two of them, but that's less likely to hurt it than my sword."

"Trust me and throw when I tell you."

Alexandra looked back, probably curious what they were talking about. Joran made a fist then opened it quickly, spreading his fingers wide.

She nodded and turned back.

Joran was pretty sure that was the symbol for an explosion, but he never was certain.

Mia had the dagger in her hand and he sensed her readiness through their link.

Now or never.

"Do it!"

Her arm whipped forward and Joran threw his vial of alchemist's fire an instant later.

The demon reacted exactly as he'd hoped.

It turned to mist to let the dagger pass through. The instant it did, his vial exploded.

The heat and shockwave blew the black mist in every direction at the same time the doors crashed open.

"Go!" Joran shouted.

They leapt through the flames and out into the hall. Imperial guards gaped at them as they appeared out of the inferno, but quickly gathered their wits enough to fall in around them.

"What's happening?" one of the guards asked.

No one bothered to answer. They needed all their strength for running.

Joran kept looking back over his shoulder for the demon or whatever it was. He doubted his trick would stop it for long.

One of the guards screamed and collapsed. Behind him, a dark claw descended from the ceiling, piercing the unfortunate man's chest.

Joran had to stop thinking in two dimensions. This thing could literally appear from anywhere.

"The exit's just ahead!" Alexandra shouted.

No dark figure appeared to try and stop them this time. Instead the invisible darkness gathered directly in front of the left-hand door.

"Guards, form a wedge and break down the doors," Joran said.

They all looked at the emperor.

"You heard him! Do it!"

A dozen imperial guards formed a wedge and rushed ahead of them. One of them went down immediately, his flesh turning pale and necrotic. The rest hit the door hard and it burst open.

The darkness shifted left.

"Everyone keep to the right side," Joran said.

The emperor and pope made it out easily. When Alexandra's turn came, a black claw reached for her head.

Joran leapt and knocked her down. A chill ran through him as the claw passed over their heads.

Mia dragged them to their feet and the group ran on through the bright sunlight. The church loomed dark, gray, and way too far in the distance. He saw no sign of the demon, but seriously doubted it had given up.

Joran dearly hoped that whatever protection the pope claimed to have turned out to be real. If it wasn't, they were all likely to die.

CHAPTER 10

"I can go no further," Grub said.

The dwarf had led Samaritan to a tiny, uncomfortably narrow side tunnel that connected to the very edge of Dwarfhome. Light and distant sounds emerged from the passage. Samaritan took his white cloak off, folded it, and handed it to Grub for safekeeping. The brown one seemed too light and its lack of alchemical enhancements made it pretty much useless for anything beyond hiding his features with the cowl.

"I'm surprised the powers that rule Dwarfhome haven't found this place yet."

"We made it with magic and no geomancer would ever help our current rulers. Most simply stay silent while others try to sneak information to the rebellion. It's seldom of any great value, but it does show we have supporters in the city. Albeit supporters that aren't willing to show their true loyalty in public."

"If they did that, they'd likely go from little value to no

value. People in prison seldom learn anything vital. Do you plan to wait here?"

Grub nodded. "I'll be safer here than anywhere else close by. You've got five days. After that, you're on your own."

"Fair enough." Samaritan pulled the silver amulet out from under his tunic. He needed to let his friend know he was coming for a visit.

Feeding ether into the metal until a glow appeared he asked, "Where are you?"

The Golden Rest inn, the same as I've been for the past several months. What about you?

"I'm about to enter Dwarfhome. I should reach your inn about an hour from now. I need your help."

Anything I can do.

Samaritan severed the connection. That was the answer he wanted to hear.

Leaving Grub, he forced his broad shoulders through the tunnel and crawled, scraping his back the entire way. Lucky for him, the connecting tunnel only ran about twenty yards before he emerged behind a two-story building. Brushing himself off, he willed the illusion that hid his scars into place and walked around the building and into the city.

Dwarfhome sat in a massive cavern probably a mile long and three-quarters that wide. The buildings had been built out of the local stone fused together with magic. Some signs of it lingered in the ether when he looked closely. He bet that when they had to fix something now, they claimed divine intervention handled the magic.

He shook his head at the mental gymnastics some people would perform. Still, when you considered the alternatives, likely a long and painful discussion with an inquisitor, that certainly justified a little playacting.

Samaritan walked along, forcing himself not to sneak or hide. He tried his best to project the idea that he belonged. That he was just another human come to take in the sights. He certainly had plenty of company. Humans and dwarves thronged through the streets, all dressed in fine, imperial-style robes. The babble of voices threatened to give him a headache.

Picking up the pace, he headed for the merchant district. Lucky for him, the rebels had made a map of the city available to him, the memory making it easy for him to find his way around. Not that asking for directions would be strange for a tourist, but he preferred not to risk it.

The crowds thinned as the buildings became fancier. Samaritan would have sworn some of them actually had gemstones studding the trim. Perhaps when you lived in an underground mining society, that served the same purpose as crown molding on the surface. He also didn't know what the city had in the way of security, but a thief wouldn't even have to actually break into a house to get rich here.

He rounded a bend and the light grew even brighter. Tall stone posts topped with giant, round alchemy lamps flooded a square with golden light almost like sunlight. Perfect, he'd finally reached the section set up for visiting surface merchants. Now, to find The Golden Rest.

He spotted it a little ways up the street past several other precious-metal-themed inns. The reason for its name became instantly apparent as the face of the building appeared to be covered from top to bottom in actual gold. Impossible of course, but the effect certainly impressed.

Three steps led up to a wraparound porch where a handful of men and women, all of them from the imperial homeland based on their skin tone and dark hair and eyes, sat drinking and having low, murmured conversations.

Samaritan would have happily murdered them all if he could've gotten away with it.

"Bellator!" a familiar voice called from behind him.

Samaritan turned to find another imperial man ambling up to him. The two men shook hands. "It's been too long."

Titus Den Cade might be the only imperial he didn't want to kill. Despite the professional disdain between their families, he and Titus had struck up a friendship their first year of college, before he decided to join the White Knights.

"Your last message said you'd be in the area, but I didn't think you'd have time to visit." Titus's smile held genuine pleasure.

"I doubted I would, but circumstances changed. Can we talk somewhere private?"

"Of course, my room's upstairs." Titus led the way inside, his sandals slapping against smooth stone.

As they walked through the packed common room, a dwarf dressed in flowing golden robes shot Samaritan a glare. His simple clothes didn't fit with the rich atmosphere, though he'd been careful to brush off all the dirt from his trip through the tunnel.

Despite his obvious distaste, the dwarf made no comment and kept his distance. Friends of the richest man in the empire —well technically that was Titus's father, but the son pretty much ran the business and everyone knew it—got away with dressing any way they wanted.

The other guests that sat eating or chatting simply ignored them as they passed. That suited Samaritan fine. The fewer people that looked at him, the happier he'd be.

A staircase at the rear of the common room led to the second floor. At the top Titus turned right and followed a short hall to a door marked with a golden one. He pushed through, revealing a suite of rooms that would have looked right at home in a Third Circle mansion.

Titus went to the nearest chair and dropped into it. "Take a seat and tell me your troubles."

Samaritan slipped his sword out of its baldric and settled easily into a leather-bound seat opposite his old friend. Whenever he spoke with Titus, it felt like those long debates they had in the student lounge years ago.

"I need information and the only place I can think to find it is the dwarven archives. My associates assure me that access is strictly controlled, but I figured if anyone can get me in, you can."

"Of course I can. The dwarves, for all their wealth and ancient culture, are still provincials. They're all eager to please a visiting noble. What do you need access to?"

"I'm looking for information on their time of enslavement to the Black Iron Empire. I believe the second beast is hidden in their territory. If the empire used the dwarves to dig or otherwise reshape the pit where it's hidden, there may be some record."

Titus scratched his chin. "Are you certain seeking another of the monsters is a good idea? From what you told me, the first one didn't work out very well."

"It didn't, but that doesn't change its potential. Besides, whoever brought it down is far from here. History will not repeat itself. When we take down the empire's richest province, it will be a powerful blow. And if I can find a clue to the location of the Black Iron Empire's capital, then we will have what we need to take the empire down permanently."

Titus nodded, a little frown creasing his forehead.

"Do you still believe in the mission?"

"Of course. The empire is a plague on the world. The lies of the church make it even worse. All people will be better off without it. I just wish there was a less destructive way to change things."

"There isn't. Destruction is the only thing they understand. We have to burn everything and start fresh. Nothing else will make things right."

Titus nodded. "Alright. We'll go to the archive tomorrow. You'll play the part of a scholar whose work we're backing. Not that I think anyone will care once they know who's asking."

"Thank you, for everything. I wouldn't have made it this far without your support. I'm sure my family appreciates it as well."

"Won't you let me tell them you survived?"

Samaritan shook his head. Bellator, the boy they knew, the son they loved, hadn't survived. All that remained was the rage- and hate-filled shell called Samaritan. "No. If the church ever learned that they knew I lived, they might use them to try and get to me. Better and safer for all of us if they never know the truth."

"I doubt they'd agree, but if you insist, I will, as always, honor your wishes. Do you have a place to spend the night?"

"I'd hoped to sleep here."

Titus's smile held a tinge of sadness. Maybe a little pity as well. Samaritan tried his best not to see it.

"Of course. The couch is quite comfortable. I have a meeting in an hour, but when I return, I'll bring food and we can catch up properly. Until then you'll find wine in the cupboard. It's a fine imperial vintage from the homeland."

Titus left and Samaritan put his feet up before closing his eyes. Sometimes he hated himself for deceiving his dear old friend. Titus truly had no idea the scope of what Samaritan and the archbishop intended to unleash. And it would have to stay that way. If he ever learned the truth, friend or not, Samaritan doubted Titus would accept the necessity despite his devotion to the cause.

Samaritan had already lost so much. If he had to lie and pretend to be a better man than he was to keep his last friend, he would do so without a second thought.

CHAPTER 11

"It's coming in from the left!" Joran shouted.

The emperor, pope, and everyone else dodged right. An especially slow guard nearly ended up impaled on the monster's claws. Two of his less-speedy comrades had already fallen, their lifeless husks still lying where they fell on the palace lawn.

Swords, spears, imperial steel or wood—nothing they hit the thing with hurt it. All of Mia's and the guards' skill meant nothing if their weapons failed to damage the enemy. Mia's frustration simmered in the back of Joran's mind, but he didn't let it get too far forward. Any distraction now might be fatal.

They'd been running for fifteen minutes for the promised safety of the church. Joran's eyes burned and tears ran down his face. He'd never looked at the ether for this long and the strain showed. And he wasn't the only one straining. He seriously doubted Septimus got much exercise. At least judging from the way he huffed and puffed. The ridiculous hat had fallen by the wayside long ago and his robe had been soaked through with sweat. Hopefully he didn't collapse before he led them to the safe room.

Only Joran's ability to see the creature when it hid in the ether allowed the group to avoid its attacks. And even with that tiny advantage they'd had some close calls. If he lost his focus and his view of the ether vanished...

No way would he let that happen. Regardless of the cost, he would maintain the magic.

As if mocking him, a new pain started screaming behind his right eye. It felt like a dozen needles stabbing him at once.

The pain nearly cost them dearly.

"Directly above you, Marcus!"

The crown prince dove out of the way at the last instant.

The guards had him on his feet and moving seconds later.

"There's the church entrance!" Alexandra said.

Thank The One God. Joran felt strange thinking the familiar prayer now that the truth had been officially revealed.

His relief vanished in an instant. The demon waited for them directly in front of the door. Its dark, cloudy form covered both sides of the entrance. They had no hope of getting past it untouched.

"Everyone stop," Joran said.

"Are you mad, boy?" Septimus said. "We're nearly safe."

The imperial family, bless them, stopped at once.

"The demon is waiting directly in front of the doors. If we try to get through, it'll carve us to pieces."

That brought the pope and cardinal to a skidding halt. The two men trudged back to the group.

"What are we going to do?" Alexandra asked.

Everyone looked at Joran as if between here and the palace he'd dreamed up some way to defeat the creature.

"The only idea I have is to use the same trick we tried in the throne room. I have one vial of alchemist's fire left. The problem is, I don't know if it will work when the demon is fully one with the ether. And even if it does, the church will sustain some damage."

"Forget that," Septimus said. "We'll just pass the plate twice next God's Day. There's always some rich idiot that thinks giving us money will help get them into heaven."

The pope's rather cynical view of his flock didn't surprise Joran. The more churchmen he met, the clearer it became that they cared less for their parishioners than they did for their coin.

"Okay," Joran said. "Let's advance slowly and see what happens. If it doesn't move, I'll try blasting it."

He moved to the front of the group with Mia right at his side. So only Joran could hear, she whispered, "Are you okay? I can feel your pain."

"The longer I maintain the ethereal link, the worse it gets. Unfortunately, there's nothing to be done about it. Until we're safe, I have to bear the discomfort."

"A stiff neck is discomfort," she said. "It feels like your brain is about to burst."

"Let's hope that doesn't happen."

Twenty feet from the door they paused again. The demon showed no sign of moving or that it feared anything they might do. That shook Joran's confidence a bit, but they really had limited options. If they didn't make it somewhere safe before the pain overwhelmed him, nothing else mattered.

He slipped the vial of alchemist's fire out of its hidden pocket and hefted it.

Here goes nothing.

His arm snapped forward and the vial exploded, dispersing the dark cloud.

"Go!"

They ran, leaping the flames and sprinting down the carpet between the pews. The pope took the lead, angling toward the right-hand door behind the altar.

Joran's gaze darted all around. As far as he could tell, the blast hadn't actually hurt the demon and he expected it to be after them in short order.

Beyond the door, the pope led them down a short hall that ended in a T. Another right brought them to a staircase leading to the basement. It would've been the perfect place for an ambush; narrow, confined, with nowhere to dodge.

They reached the stone floor without issue. He thought the demon hadn't been hurt. It certainly didn't look like the alchemist's fire had done any damage. Of course, the more he learned, the more he understood just how deep his ignorance of alchemy's underlying principles ran.

Septimus took a left this time and after a few strides brought them to a halt in front of a blank stone wall. Since Joran doubted the pope was a total idiot, he assumed a concealed door would allow them to proceed.

Sure enough, a couple touches on barely noticeable bumps in the wall and a stone door dropped out of sight. The group hurried through into a chamber about the size of Alexandra's closet. They all stopped and stared.

In the center of it, a shining sword gleamed under an alchemical light. More perfect and pure than even Joran's platinum amulet, he'd never seen such a perfectly made item.

Behind him one of the guards at the rear of the group screamed.

Joran didn't even have to look to know what caused it.

"Get closer to the sword," Septimus said.

He needn't have bothered as everyone immediately crowded away from the entrance where the demon lurked.

Joran spun in time to see the creature resume its physical form. It took two steps into the room, snarled, and stopped cold. The sword's circle of protection seemed to extend about five paces in every direction. Not exactly a huge space, but at least they seemed to be safe for the moment.

"How long do you think you can cower around that sword?" the demon asked. "You'll have to leave eventually and when you do, I'll be waiting."

It vanished into the ether and drifted beyond Joran's sight. Before he released the magic, he studied the sword. Where the demon's aura had been black and twisted, the sword gave off a pure, white, ethereal light. The pain in his head eased just looking at it.

At last he released the spell and closed his eyes. Tears ran down his cheeks. He brushed them away and when he opened his eyes found his hand bloody. You didn't need to be a master healer to know that tears of blood were a bad sign.

Alexandra sat and said, "You need to rest. Lie down."

Joran had absolutely no intention of arguing. Mia helped him down and he laid his head on Alexandra's lap. That felt heavenly.

"Where did you get this sword?" the emperor asked.

"It's the church's most holy artifact," Septimus said. "The last relic of the Prophet's. He carried this sword when he arrived in Tiber. Everything else rotted away, but this hasn't changed in over five hundred years. One of my predecessors had this room built. Some alchemy stuff in the stand lets the sword expand its protective aura a few extra feet. I haven't the slightest idea what it is or how it works, but I'm glad it turned out not to be another mad fancy."

"I second that," Marcus said. "But the fact remains that the demon was right. We can't stay here forever. What are we going to do?"

"When my eyes are recovered," Joran said. "Mia is going to take up that sword and kill the demon with it."

"I am?" Mia asked.

"You're the only one I can share my sight with, not to mention you're the best sword fighter we've got. I'm sure you can do it."

"There's a small problem with your plan," Rufious said. "If she takes the sword, we lose its protection."

"Two days without water and we'll be too weak to even try and fight it. Two or maybe three days after that, we'll all be dead." Joran turned his head a fraction to look at Rufious. "If that's your preference, fine, but I doubt the rest of us want to die with our tongues stuck to the roofs of our mouths, swollen to three times its normal size."

Rufious grimaced but offered no more objections.

"What do you need?" the emperor asked.

"A few hours to rest. Wake me at least an hour before sunset. Fighting this thing after dark isn't a prospect that interests me."

Mia knelt and took his hand. "Can I really do this?"

"I've shared my sight with you once already. The second time should be easier. As for killing the demon, if you can't do it, none of us can. All I've got left is one vial of adhesive and one of acid. Not the most impressive of arsenals."

"If I screw up, the empire is doomed."

Joran squeezed her hand. "You won't. And even if you do, take comfort in the fact that we'll all be too dead to care."

A short, hysterical giggle slipped out and Joran felt Mia's fear go with it. Just as he'd hoped.

At last, she lay down beside him, resting her head on his shoulder. A second later they both fell fast asleep.

CHAPTER 12

Samaritan made sure to follow a respectful distance behind Titus as they walked through the streets of Dwarfhome. Today he played the part of a scholar funded by the Den Cade family. He and Titus drew little more than a passing glance from the dwarves marching here and there on their way to do whatever city-dwelling dwarves did. He hadn't seen much in the way of carts or beasts of burden. Samaritan assumed they had some. Perhaps they were kept away from the areas frequented by the wealthy and powerful. That struck him as the sort of thing a people determined to impress their perceived betters might do.

Their destination, the dwarven archive, sat to the left of the governor's mansion, unattached but close enough for the local guards to keep a close eye on whoever came and went. No doubt it would also make it easy to deal with any unwelcome visitors.

The main thoroughfare through Dwarfhome ran from the main gates that allowed access to visitors from the surface to the government compound. Speaking of which, he spotted the three-story mansion ahead of them. Tiny figures marched along the top of the wall surrounding the compound. Light glinted off their imperial steel axes.

Another dozen stood around the front of the gate, a great, steel portcullis that looked strong enough to withstand any normal assault. No doubt some sort of alchemy would make short work of it, but Samaritan hadn't gotten that far in his studies. He'd learned most of the basics, but he wasn't even close to master level to say nothing of grandmaster.

As they drew closer Titus said, "Remind me again what you're researching?"

"The Black Iron Empire, specifically as it relates to the dwarves. It might be best not to mention any interest in their time of enslavement."

"Of course. Even provincials have their pride. Best let me handle things until we reach the archive."

Inside, Samaritan wondered if even Titus's pull would be enough to get them in. Still he nodded and made no comment. If the Den Cade name failed to open the door, he didn't know what he'd do next. Violence had no hope of success, at least an assault by one man didn't. If he had an army, that would be another matter.

Of course, if he had an army, he wouldn't need giant beasts to do his work for him.

Titus stopped in front of the gate guards who now hefted their axes as if hoping for the chance to use them. Probably just for show. Anyone visiting the government compound likely numbered among the rich and powerful. Exactly the sort you wouldn't want to intimidate.

These dwarves made Grub look like an underfed orphan. They all had massive shoulders and chests covered in mail.

Dark beards hung below steel helms. Hard eyes glittered in the shadows cast by the helms.

One of the dwarves moved to stand in the fore. He had a silver hammer symbol centered on his helm. A rank indicator of some sort, though Samaritan had no idea what it meant.

"Can I help you, sir?" Silver Hammer asked.

"I hope so," Titus said. "My name is Titus Den Cade and this gentleman with me is a scholar in my employ. We need access to the archive. My family is funding his research."

"Access to the archive is highly restricted. You'll need the governor's permission."

"I understand. I'm sure if you send a messenger, Governor Bramrule will tell you to let us in. He did mention the last time we had dinner that if I needed anything, I should just ask."

"You know the governor?" Silver Hammer's voice held a good deal more respect now.

"Very well. We've been meeting regularly for the past few months." Titus smiled. "If we don't make a deal soon, the man's appetite is apt to bankrupt me."

The guards all chuckled at that.

Silver Hammer turned and said, "One of you lot run up and tell the governor Lord Den Cade is here and that he wants to visit the archive."

The dwarf with the shortest beard slammed the haft of his axe on the portcullis and once it clanked up ducked under and hurried toward the mansion.

Titus had always had a talent for manipulating people and it seemed the skill hadn't dulled. It made him a great merchant, but during his college days, Samaritan had argued it made him corrupt. Now he understood it was simply how the world worked. Everyone used everyone else, churchmen included. He thought no more of manipulating people to get what he needed than he did killing them. As long as his mission succeeded, nothing else mattered.

It took nearly half an hour for the stocky guard to return. The run didn't seem to have tired him out.

"Well?" Silver Hammer asked.

"Governor Bramwell says Lord Den Cade and his companion are to have whatever access they require for as long as they require and we shouldn't bother him again."

Silver Hammer grimaced then shrugged. "Well, that's cleared up. We'll put your name on the approved list should you come when a different shift is on duty. Raise the gate!"

The portcullis clanked up, Titus nodded to the guards, and Samaritan followed him inside the compound. And just like that they were inside. The power of the nobility on display for all to see. Samaritan hated it even as he appreciated the convenience.

They ignored the mansion and made their way to the rather plain, two-story building next door. The only thing that marked it as the archive was the scroll symbol over the door. No scholars waited outside. Nor did any guards for that matter. You'd think someone would be interested in the history of their people.

When Samaritan mentioned it Titus shrugged. "All the dwarves I've dealt with tend to be forward looking. They want to make a better, and by that I mean richer, tomorrow. They don't care to think about their past, except as a series of mistakes to avoid in the future."

Samaritan stopped. "If that's true, why were they so eager to join the empire? I mean, they'd already been enslaved by one empire."

"Exactly. Think how our empire—"

"It is *not* my empire."

"I know, I know. I'm simply calling it that to distinguish it from the Black Iron Empire. My point is, consider how we treat a province that joins willingly, even eagerly, and how we treat one that resists. The dwarves are now richer and more powerful than when they were an independent kingdom. From their point of view, the decision has been a fantastic success."

"The rebels and geomancers wouldn't agree."

Titus looked around. "I'm on your side, remember? Anyway, this might not be the best subject to discuss in the open surrounded by the seat of the provincial government."

Samaritan forced his jaw to relax. "Of course not. I sometimes lose my focus when the subject comes up. After you."

The two men walked up the short flight of steps to the landing. Titus tried the door and it opened easily. Inside, an entry area of gray stone lit by a single alchemical light sat empty. At the rear of the room a bar, for Samaritan could think of nothing else to call it, blocked access to the rest of the archive.

"This is the strangest library I've ever seen," Titus said. "And the emptiest."

They advanced to the bar. "Hello?" Titus called.

No answer.

He tried pounding on the bar and got the same response.

"What is this, a self-serve archive?" Titus asked.

Samaritan leaned over the bar and looked left and right. About ten paces down from where they stood, an unconscious dwarf slept curled around a brown clay bottle.

"I think I found the librarian."

Titus leaned over beside him. "You've got to be kidding. Even if we wake him up, he won't be worth a damn for hours. Clearly no one comes to the archive. Can you find what you need on your own?"

Samaritan shrugged. "If there's a catalogue, probably. If not, no way."

"We might as well take a look. Do you see any way back there besides jumping the bar?"

Samaritan chuckled. "We haven't jumped a bar since our college days. Hang on."

A little ways down the bar he spotted a switch. At his touch, a click sounded and a section of bar popped up. Titus lifted it and led the way into the archive. Shelf after shelf of tablets filled the space. Tiny runes covered each of them from top to bottom. Samaritan's eyes ached just looking at them.

Out of curiosity, he pulled one of the tablets off its shelf and nearly dropped it. Damn thing had to weigh close to fifty pounds.

"There's a table over here," Titus said.

Samaritan lugged his tablet over and eased it down on a two-foot-tall table. He peered closer in the dim light and swore. The runes were Dwarven. He didn't know how to read Dwarven. He did know how to use translation magic, but that would exhaust him after a few hours. To make matters worse, he only had four days left to rejoin Grub. Nothing short of angry dwarves armed with crossbows could make his situation worse.

"I'm going to take a quick look at this one," Samaritan said. "I know you have other things that require your attention, but if you'd take a look around for anything resembling a catalogue before you left, it would help me a ton."

"Sure," Titus said. "I've got half an hour before my next meeting. I can spare fifteen minutes."

His friend wandered down the path between bookcases and Samaritan sat on the floor beside the table. No way did humans ever visit here. This table barely felt tall enough for a dwarf. And where were the chairs?

Shaking off the irrelevant questions, Samaritan drew threads of ether through the tablet and into his eyes. As he did so, he commanded the words to appear in Imperial. The runes resisted for a few seconds, but soon enough they wavered and melted into Imperial script. Not wanting to waste too much time on irrelevant information, he skimmed the text.

A minute later he dismissed the spell. The tablet discussed the first dwarves to reach the surface and how quickly they fled back into the earth. Useless, worthless information. He lugged the tablet back to the shelf that held it and with much grunting and swearing shoved it back in place.

That's when he noticed the little marks on the edge of the tablets.

Renewing his spell, he read the marks. They were dates. That explained the shelving system. They went by date rather than subject. Far from ideal, but at least he'd know where to start his search. The Black Iron Empire fell about six hundred or so years ago. The giant beasts were created toward the end of the empire, at least based on the little he'd learned about them.

That argued for seven hundredish years ago.

"I didn't find a catalogue," Titus said as he approached. Samaritan had been so caught up in his thinking he didn't even notice his friend's footsteps. Not great if an enemy had been in the area. "But I did find a map of the archive."

Titus handed him a scroll of blessedly light paper. It said exactly where to find what it called the Era of Enslavement. That would have the information he needed. While it covered an uncomfortably long period, at least he had a starting point.

"This is very helpful, thank you, Titus."

"Glad to be of use. Will you be returning to the inn tonight?"

"Unless they kick me out, I'll sleep here. I don't want to waste any time. Likely I won't see you again before I find the weapon. Before I wake it, I'll send a warning."

"Much appreciated, old friend." Titus clapped him on the shoulder. "And good luck."

Samaritan nodded, his mind already racing as he considered where to start looking. Even if he found the hidden pit, he still needed a soulbound pair to wake the monster from its slumber. They weren't exactly common among the dwarves, not that they were common anywhere else.

Maybe the archbishop could help. She had agents all over the place.

He shook his head. Time enough to worry about that later. He needed to start reading.

CHAPTER 13

Joran's eyes had started working properly again and the blood no longer leaked down his cheeks. He still wanted to take a yearlong nap, but given their rather precarious situation, that would have to wait.

With great reluctance, he sat up, leaving the comfort of Alexandra's lap behind. Both she and Mia gave him worried looks. Everyone else just looked worried in general.

"Are you certain you rested long enough?" Alexandra asked.

"Not in the least, but time isn't on our side. Who knows what chaos that creature might be getting up to while we sit here, protected by the Prophet's sword? No, I fear the time has come to get back into the fight. Ready, Mia?"

"As I'll ever be." His soulmate helped him up and they went over to the sword.

Septimus stood in the way. "You can't take the church's most holy relic. Not to mention the only thing standing between us and that demon."

"It's not a holy artifact," Joran pointed out. "The Prophet

was a fraud, you said so yourself. And the sword will still be between you and the demon, it will just be in Mia's hand instead."

"Enough arguing, Septimus," the emperor said. "The situation is as clear to you as it is to the rest of us. We won't be safe until the demon is slain. Having seen Mia in battle, I'm confident she can handle the task, especially with Joran backing her up. All the rest of us have to do is stay close and out of the way. Even you should be able to manage that."

The pope muttered something that sounded distinctly like a curse he remembered his father using, but only when Mother was out of earshot. Definitely not holy language.

After a staring contest with the emperor he had no hope of winning, Septimus threw up his hands. "Fine, we can all die together. Best of luck, young lady."

He moved out of the way and Joran and Mia took the final steps to the stand.

She reached for the sword then hesitated. "What if he's right? What if I can't do this?"

"You killed a giant serpent, a demon can't be that much harder. Have a little faith in yourself. At least as much faith as I have in you."

"You're absolutely certain I can kill that thing?" she asked, disbelief clear in her tone.

"Of course. You've saved the day enough times that I'm certain you'll do it again. If you can't have faith in yourself, then have faith that I know what you can do better than you do. Now, grab that sword and let's go kill a demon."

Mia took a deep breath, reached out, and grasped the sword. In one smooth motion she drew it and spun to face the door. Not that the demon would have to come from that way, but at least she seemed to have slipped into battle mode rather than nervous, uncertain mode. If they had to fight a demon, Joran vastly preferred that one.

"How does it feel?" he asked.

"Amazing. The balance is perfect. It almost seems to float in my hand. I've never felt anything like it."

"Excellent." Joran shifted his vision so the ether appeared. He found he could do it now without much mental effort. Maintaining it, on the other hand, still drained him. Sharing his vision with Mia would take even more out of him.

But fighting an invisible demon would be too much even for her.

Concentrating on their link, Joran willed his vision to join with hers. Something happened in the either and now he literally saw out of Mia's eyes. He also saw the ether, so that part worked at least. Now, how to leave the magical vision behind and return his sight to his body?

"Are we staying or going?" Septimus asked.

"I'm working on it," Joran said. He didn't want to snap at the pope, but he lacked the focus to worry about diplomacy.

He closed his eyes and willed his sight back but the magical vision to stay. When he opened his eyes, he found the ether still visible.

"Can you still see the magic?" Joran asked.

"Yes," she said in awe. "It's so beautiful."

"You need to kind of ignore the pretty and focus on the darkness. That will be the demon."

"Right, okay, I'm ready."

Given what he felt through their link, he seriously doubted that, but wouldn't say anything that might undermine whatever modest amount of confidence she'd gained. Instead he focused on sending Mia positive thoughts. If he believed in her, hopefully she'd believe in herself.

Joran opened the door and motioned her out first. When everyone had passed him, he followed at the rear. Between them, they should be able to see anything trying to sneak up on the group. They made it up and out of the church without issue. As far as Joran could tell, the demon hadn't harmed anyone, at least it hadn't left any bodies lying around.

The alchemist's fire had burned out while they were in the basement, leaving behind blackened stone. At least it didn't appear to have done any structural damage.

"So what now?" Septimus asked. "We wander around in the dark until it attacks again?"

"You're welcome to stay here and pray for The One God's protection," the emperor said. "Let's make our way to the palace. If it wants that cursed sword, maybe we can force a confrontation there."

Joran dearly hoped so. After only five minutes, his headache had already returned. Earlier it had taken nearly an hour to get this bad. Assuming it grew worse at the same accelerated rate, he figured they had at most an hour before the pain rendered him unconscious.

Mia must have sensed it through their link as she set a brisk pace back toward the palace. His best guess put the time at an hour before sunset. Nevertheless, the streets were quiet. Just as well for them as more people only meant more targets for the demon. When they reached the main entrance, the guards on duty instantly opened the doors and averted their gaze as the emperor passed.

"I'm not sure where to go next," Mia said.

Marcus glanced at Alexandra, but she shook her head.

Joran appreciated her desire to stay by his side. In fifteen minutes, he might be in serious need of someone to hang on to.

"I'll show you the way." Marcus moved to the front of the line beside Mia. It looked like he'd rather be just about anywhere else.

Joran understood that feeling all too well. Yet he'd at least gotten to choose his fate. Marcus simply had the luck, good or bad depending on your point of view, to have been born heir to the throne.

"Guards, you will wait here," the emperor said.

"Your Imperial Majesty—" One of them started to argue, but the emperor raised his hand.

"This danger isn't one you can protect me from. Whatever happens from here, your presence or absence will not affect it one way or the other."

Pained but obedient, the guards brought their fists to their hearts. Joran considered himself a loyal citizen, but he wouldn't have been pained to be left behind had his presence not been needed. He tried and failed to imagine what sort of indoctrination program they used on the imperial guards.

The group set out once more. Joran focused as intensely as he ever had through the many twists and turns. Marcus led them through back passages Joran hadn't even known existed before they finally reached a staircase leading to the basement. At the bottom waited a long, unguarded passage with a massive steel door at the end.

Still no sign of the demon. Did the demon fear Mia's sword? He hoped so. That meant it thought they might be able to hurt it.

Joran's actual vision had grown blurry though the ether

remained clear. Hopefully the demon worked up the courage to do something soon.

"That must be the vault," Joran said.

"Indeed," the emperor said. "You should all be honored. Usually only members of the imperial family have access to this place.

Joran felt many things, most of them painful and none of them honored.

A short walk brought them to the vault door. Joran leaned against the wall and rested his eyes a moment. While they were closed, someone did something to open the vault.

Alexandra took his hand. "We're almost there."

He squeezed back, opened his eyes, and followed the others inside.

The vault held a number of shiny, golden treasures on stands and shelves. The black sword sat alone on a table well away from the other items. It looked like whoever brought it here feared it might taint everything else by proximity. Judging by the darkness it threw off in the ether, they might not have been wrong.

"We're here," Septimus asked. "What now? The creature is clearly terrified of the Prophet's sword. Are we supposed to wait around forever?"

The pope drew glares from all three members of the imperial family and even Rufious looked disgusted. But for all his whining, Septimus had a point. If it waited too long, they'd be just as helpless as they were before.

They needed to draw it in for a final confrontation. And he had an idea how to do that, assuming the silver sword did what he thought.

"Do you care if the black sword is destroyed, Majesty?"

Joran asked. He didn't even use the emperor's full title in mixed company. Even worse, he was so tired he didn't care.

"Not in the least," the emperor said. "The thing is clearly cursed. If you don't destroy it, I'm going to have it shipped to the coast to be dumped in the deepest part of the ocean."

"Mia, touch it with your sword. Keep the two in contact."

"What will that do?" Alexandra asked.

"If I'm right, it will negate the sword's dark aura. Assuming that aura is essential to its existence, it will eventually destroy it. More importantly, there's no way a creature that can merge with the magic will miss what we're doing. Assuming it actually wants the sword as badly as it seems to, it will have to attack or lose its prize."

"Will it hurt the Prophet's sword?" Septimus asked.

Joran shrugged. His knees wobbled and he nearly fell. Only Alexandra's hand on his back kept him upright.

"Let's find you a place to rest." Alexandra helped him over to an empty stretch of wall and they sat together.

Mia brushed the pope aside, her determination coming through their link loud and clear. Joran managed a weak smile. Anything that threatened his wellbeing served as a catalyst for her. Not that he had any intention of walking into danger without need, but it came as a relief to know that if he had to, it would bring out her best.

"What's got you so happy?" Alexandra asked. "You look like death warmed over."

Joran nodded toward Mia as she prepared to touch the silver sword to the black one. "She's focused now. All her doubts and fear are gone. When the demon arrives, she'll cut it to pieces."

When the tip of the silver sword reached an inch separating

it from the black one, Joran sent a prayer heavenward. Even if The One God was a lie, hopefully some greater power watched over them. And if said power served the side of mortals, maybe it would send a little luck Mia's way.

The silver sword touched the black one and a rush of power blasted through the ether. If the demon didn't see that, then it had to be blind.

———

At first, the weird, swirling lights had made Mia's head spin. If Joran saw them and made some sense of what they meant, she didn't know how. Of course, she didn't know how Joran did many of the things he did. But she knew for sure he was in pain, and her questions and doubts did nothing to help him feel better. So she put them in the little box in the back of her mind where she shoved her fear before a fight.

If she needed to defeat a demon to help Joran, then she would fight and kill the thing without mercy.

The tip of the silver sword touched the flat of the black one and a wave of power rushed over her. White light from her sword seemed to consume the darkness.

Mia pressed harder. If she broke the black sword, that would surely draw out the demon. Her lips drew back as she bore down.

Was a crack forming in the blood groove?

"Above you!" Joran shouted with all his limited strength.

She didn't think.

Instinct made her leap back and swing the sword in front of her.

The edge passed through an arm made of black smoke. The piece she cut off vanished in a puff of darkness.

The demon's crimson eyes flashed. Either she'd hurt it or just made it angry.

A dozen claws shot out from the cloud of darkness.

Mia dodged and slashed, avoiding some while severing others.

While less dramatic than her battle with the giant serpent, fighting a thing without substance that could attack her in so many ways from so many directions offered an even greater challenge.

The fact that it seemed no matter how many arms she severed, it did the demon no real harm made things even more difficult. It wasn't like a cloud of darkness had a head to chop off or a heart to pierce. Mia had a lot of skill when it came to killing living opponents, but the demon had her totally outclassed.

The darkness shifted toward the emperor and his son.

Mia darted between them and the demon and slashed, driving it back. "Your fight is with me, monster."

Joran's presence in the back of her mind strengthened. When it did, a dense ball of darkness appeared near the center of the demon's mass. That had to be its heart.

He'd showed that to her, and now his pain had increased again.

Mia had no more time to waste. Her soulmate had given her everything she needed to beat this thing. Time to stop fooling around and finish it.

She charged, sword leading like a lance.

Claw-tipped arms came at her from every direction.

Dodging and slashing, Mia bore in.

No more retreat. This time, one of them would fall.

The demon had other ideas. It flew back and up toward the ceiling.

Mia refused to let it get away.

She kicked off the pedestal holding the black sword and swung.

A shadowy claw grazed her left arm and it went numb.

The pain didn't break her focus and the silver sword passed through the clot of darkness at its heart. Again she felt no resistance, but the dark cloud exploded, filling her with nausea.

Mia landed lightly and struggled to keep the contents of her stomach inside. Her left arm hung limp and useless at her side. All around the vault the lights and darkness had vanished. That had to mean they won.

She ignored everything else and hurried over to Joran. His psychic pain nearly overwhelmed her. She'd never seen him so pale. Blood trickled out of his eyes and stained Alexandra's dress. The princess seemed either unaware of or uninterested in the fact.

"Told you that you could do it," he said, his voice so soft she barely heard.

"Only because you showed me where to hit it. Will you be okay?"

"Need to rest." She sensed he had something else to say and leaned in closer. He whispered, "Don't let them have the sword back. We'll need it."

He fell unconscious and Mia swallowed. How did he expect her to stop the pope of all people from taking back the sword?

Her good hand tightened on the hilt. If Joran said they'd need it, she'd stop him, even if it meant removing his head from his body.

"Is it over?" the emperor asked.

"It is." Mia stood and rotated her left shoulder. Some of the feeling had already returned.

"Then I'll take our sword back," the pope said.

"No. Joran said we'll need it."

"I'm not asking you, girl, I'm telling you. Give it to me."

Mia's eyes narrowed. If not for her and Joran, this arrogant fool would be dead. How dare he start giving orders like he had something to say about what happened.

"I'm not giving it to you and if you'd like to try and take it, you're welcome to do so."

The pope sputtered something inarticulate and turned to the emperor. "I demand you order her to give it back."

The emperor looked at Mia and shook his head. "It's in good hands, Septimus, and frankly, even if I ordered her to give the sword to you, I doubt she'd obey. And seeing as how we all owe our lives to those two, a little forbearance wouldn't be a bad thing. Why don't you go back to the church and get those books we discussed ready? I'll send someone to pick them up in the morning."

With her enhanced hearing, Mia thought she heard the pope's teeth grinding. Pointing out that the being from which you derive all your authority wasn't real played hell with the pecking order. It seemed what little respect the imperial family held for the pope had run out.

"Fine!" Septimus spun and stalked toward the door. Halfway there he paused and turned back. "But this isn't over."

He and Cardinal Rufious had almost reached the door when the emperor called back, "And remember not to leave any of them out."

The pope's curse would have done a teamster proud. As holy men went, he seemed like one of the less holy ones.

"That was tremendously satisfying." The emperor looked down at Joran's unconscious form. "We need to get that young man somewhere safe and comfortable. He is a treasure greater than anything in the vault. As are you, Mia."

He added that last with a smile.

Mia didn't know how to react, so she bowed and stayed silent. Compliments from the emperor made her uncomfortable. Actually, compliments from anyone made her uncomfortable. She'd barely gotten used to Joran saying nice things about her and not wanting something in return.

"I suppose we'll need to bring a couple guards down here to carry him back to your suite, Alexandra," the emperor carried on as if oblivious to her discomfort. "I hate to let anyone see what's down here, but if I can't trust my own personal guards…"

His tone made it clear that he didn't trust his guards, not completely.

"I can carry him to the end of the hall, Majesty," Mia said. "Then you can lock the door and no one will see your treasures."

"Splendid, you do that and we'll find the guards. Come along, Marcus."

The emperor and his eldest son strode out of the vault, leaving Mia and Alexandra alone with Joran. He looked so helpless lying there.

"Are we asking too much of him?" Alexandra brushed her hand through Joran's hair. It was such a caring gesture Mia hardly believed the princess capable of it. "I know Father wants to use him until there's nothing left then marry me off to some other nobleman I'll probably hate. It would be horrible beyond measure to find someone you love only to lose them."

Mia knew exactly how she felt. She bent and scooped Joran up off Alexandra's bloodstained lap. He seemed too light, like something had been sucked out of him.

"I can carry him the whole way."

Alexandra only nodded. "I'll lock the vault and catch up with you."

Mia made her way down the empty hall. Her left arm felt mostly recovered. Hopefully Joran would be equally recovered soon.

CHAPTER 14

Fane strode through the halls of her citadel toward the casting chamber where she worked her most difficult spells. Once a month, without fail, she used a scrying spell to search for the Black Iron Empire's capital. She'd been doing it for centuries with no luck and if she was honest with herself, she would have admitted that the capital likely lay outside the range of her spell.

But she refused to admit that. It would mean that she was now fully reliant on Samaritan finding some clue that had eluded her. Fane hated relying on anyone or anything she didn't fully control. Lord Sur had warned her on many occasions that only a fool did otherwise. And so she would seek, likely in vain.

Ten strides from the chamber a pain stabbed through her immortal body. Not her pain, but the pain of her creation dying. Somehow the primitive alchemists of the Tiberian Empire had figured out a way to kill her most powerful creation. That struck her at once as impossible, but denying reality made her the fool. Clearly she had underestimated her opponents.

The pain passed as the mist wraith fully dissolved. Years of work gone without a trace. She shook her head. What a waste. And even worse, she had no more servants capable of picking up where the wraith left off. Though galling, she'd have to write the black iron sword off as a loss. She'd certainly be more careful about loaning out the other three.

A few seconds brought her to her casting chamber. It measured twenty feet by twenty feet square and in the center a smooth pool of Black Bile filled a depression about six feet across. Corrupt power crackled in her magical vision. The ooze held so much power and it represented only the smallest fraction of the dragon's true might. Her research indicated that the bile was basically the beast's sweat. Imagine what its blood and scales could do. When she mastered it, no one would ever oppose her again.

Always *when*, never *if*, though *if* might well be the more accurate assessment.

Fane conjured a pad of corrupt ether and sat inches above the dark pool. Its power immediately rose up through her, charging her undead body with energy. She closed her eyes and freed her mind. When she saw her body below her, Fane dove down through the pool.

As she always did, she followed the pipe down into the earth until it turned and leveled out. After a minute or so she reached the first lake of bile. Rising up out of it she gazed down at the thousands of gallons of the stuff that filled the low cavern. She'd found dozens of these lakes in her explorations, all of them feeding a sprawling system of pipes that carried Black Bile all through the continent.

For hundreds or more likely thousands of years the dragon

had been excreting the ooze. If only they had some way to access the power and keep it stable. She almost wouldn't need the dragon then. Unfortunately, Beastmaster was right about one thing: any time you used too much Black Bile, the results turned too chaotic to be of real use.

It even corrupted the ether to such an extent that she had trouble orienting herself. Finally, she got a rough idea which way the ocean lay and dove back into the lake, seeking a pipe that ran in the correct direction.

When she found it, Fane rushed along to the west at break-neck speed. She took every left-hand branch until she emerged in yet another bile lake. This cavern measured at least twice as big as the first one she visited. It also represented the furthest east she'd managed to reach. No pipes exited in that direction from here. North and south had yielded nothing of interest during her many searches.

Curious, she flew straight up through the cavern ceiling until she emerged, invisible, on the surface. About twenty miles in the distance, she spotted the ocean. She flew toward it, intent on searching for something that ran under the water. Everything she'd learned suggested that the Black Iron Empire's capital lay across the ocean to the east.

Even if she got that part right, the ocean was a big place and she had no real idea where to search other than to the east.

Less than a mile from where she emerged her spirit jerked to a stop. Even with the Black Bile enhancing her magic, the thread couldn't extend any further. She instinctively understood that if she pushed any further the thread would break and her spirit would never return to her body.

Having no desire to spend the rest of eternity as a disembodied spirit, Fane stopped pushing. Instead, she looked around, trying to fix her location in her mind. Given her body's rather dangerous limits where sunlight was involved, she seldom left the safety of her citadel, but that's why she had agents.

She just needed to figure out where to send them.

Spinning in a slow circle, Fane searched for something specific. She found it a moment later. A spark of corruption about five miles from the ocean. It resembled Black Bile in her magical vision, but on the surface. Maybe a bile spring had formed. That would be easy for her people to find. Smiling to herself, she willed her spirit back to her body.

Unlike the journey east, her return happened in an instant. Fane closed her eyes and waited for her spirit to fully connect once more to her body. When she extended her spirit to its very limit, she always felt a little hollow on her return. Lord Sur had warned her when he taught her the spell not to use it too often lest she begin to lose fine motor control permanently.

Fane limited her explorations to once a month for exactly that reason. Fine motor control was absolutely vital for a wizard.

Opening her eyes, she made a few experimental movements. Everything seemed good. Satisfied, she stepped off the ethereal platform and strode out of her casting chamber. Time to see if her good-for-nothing overseer had the ability to redeem himself.

———

Overseer paced around his new, much diminished base. The ruined fort had been destroyed by bandits a century ago and never rebuilt. The empire had found a better place near a new trade route to build the replacement. After his recent string of failures, he only had two teams under his command. Two teams to work the archbishop's will in the imperial homeland. An impossible situation for even the most skilled overseer, which he considered himself.

He'd done everything right. His mistress couldn't hold him responsible because his teams failed. Overseer would have smiled had his half-melted face allowed it. He understood how the archbishop thought and he knew she held him fully responsible for everything his underlings did. That's why she gave him a modicum of free will when she created him.

If he failed to do better in the future, he doubted his existence would continue for long.

At the edge of the training yard he turned and took a step back toward the opposite side. A moment later the heavy weight of his mistress's awareness settled on him. Overseer swallowed. He hadn't spoken to her since she dismissed him from her presence at the citadel. At least he had no new failures to report.

He stopped and focused. "Mistress?"

What resources remain to you?

"I have two teams. One to the north of Tiber acting as bandits and another to the west waiting for new orders. I'm uncertain what to have them do next."

I know exactly what to have them do next. You will take them to investigate a potential new bile spring. Alert me at once when you've secured the location. I'll come see for myself.

A location far from the imperial homeland burned itself into his mind. Overseer had never gone so far from his area of operation. The thought of that as well as acting directly sent a shudder through him. He'd been designed to stay hidden and act through others. Everything in him screamed that going personally would be a grave mistake.

Not that he said any of this to the archbishop. To her he said, "I will depart at once, Mistress."

Do not fail me again.

With that her presence vanished. She'd made no direct threat and didn't need to. Overseer understood perfectly well what would happen should he fail her again. Though his heart hadn't beat in many years, he found his chest tightened as if it did.

CHAPTER 15

Samaritan's shoulders burned as he lugged another of the stone tablets back to his far-too-short table. And despite how bad his shoulders ached, his eyes weren't much better. The translation spell, when held for long periods, gave him double vision and a splitting headache. After three days of constant reading, he had certainly held the spell for too long.

At least no one had bothered him. The drunk dwarf he assumed worked as some sort of librarian staggered off the first morning without so much as a word of acknowledgment. No way had the dwarf been drunk enough not to notice the hourly thuds of tablets hitting tabletop. He appeared to simply not care. Not the sort of attitude Samaritan had expected from the person in charge of the archive, but he had no intention of complaining. The fewer people who knew what information he sought, the better.

Now for his most recent effort. Turning his gaze on the tablet he let the magic flow through his eyes, winced as what felt like a needle stabbed him in the left temple, and started reading. He'd been focused on the narrative of a dwarven historian who made recording their time held captive to the Back Iron Empire his life's work. Samaritan had started at the end and worked his way back. So far he'd read through the last fifty years of the empire and figured he had to be getting close to what he sought.

With only two days remaining until Grub left him to his own devices, he'd better be.

Samaritan read for the next hour and his excitement grew. While the description of the location was vague, this had to be what he sought. Now, where was it?

He bore down, ignoring the growing discomfort, and read every word lest he miss some vital clue. At last, he found it three paragraphs from the end. The dwarves had been ordered to dig a pit five hundred feet deep and a hundred feet across. Thousands of slaves had worked on the project and scores died in the process.

When at last the masters were satisfied, they brought a bubble of darkness so big it nearly didn't fit through the opening. The bubble dropped out of sight and the slaves got to work filling the pit back in. Every few feet an imperial wizard would fuse the broken rock into solid stone. When at last they finished, it looked like the pit had never existed. The weary slaves began the long walk back to Dwarfhome.

Three days from the pit, every slave save one ended up slaughtered. The surviving dwarf played dead for two days to make sure the masters wouldn't return. He lived just long enough to share his story with the person that told the story to the author of this history.

Samaritan had read something about a memorial to the slaves' murder on that first tablet. If he found that spot, it shouldn't be too hard to locate the buried beast. Waking it would be another matter, but he refused to contact the arch-bishop until he'd found exactly what he sought.

He slid the slab he just finished back into its slot and returned to the very first one. A couple minutes later he found the passage about the memorial. He read it three times to make sure he wouldn't forget any details and at last released the spell.

His eyes nearly wept with relief. Leaving the final tablet for the librarian to put back, he retraced his steps to the archive entrance. He saw no one in any direction, shrugged, and stepped out into the cavern.

Pausing to scratch his cheek, he swore. Samaritan had forgotten to restore the illusion hiding his scars.

"Did you find everything you wanted?" Silver Hammer, the dwarf from the front gate, waved at him as he marched closer. He seemed far friendlier now that he knew Samaritan rubbed elbows with the great and powerful.

Samaritan struggled to restore the simple spell. He'd used so much ether over the past three days that he had trouble casting. The dwarf stood only a few paces away when it finally settled into place.

Swallowing a sigh he nodded. "Yes, thank you. Lord Den Cade will be most pleased when I tell him everything I learned. Though I must say your librarian leaves something to be desired."

"That's for sure. He's a drunk, but also the governor's nephew, so we're stuck with him. At least he stays out of the way for the most part. The boys will let you out with our compliments to your employer."

"I'll be sure to extend your compliments. Good evening."

"Good morning. It's about midday surface time."

Samaritan stared. Had he so totally lost track of time?

"How long have I been in there?"

"A little over five days. I debated sending a rescue party to check on you, but didn't—"

"Excuse me. I'm very late for an important engagement." Samaritan took off running. If Grub had already left, then heaven help him.

———

The trip through Dwarfhome seemed to take forever, but Samaritan didn't dare slow down. Nothing could go wrong now that he finally had the information he needed. Once he would have prayed that Grub gave him a little more time than he promised, but now he just hoped and saved his breath for walking.

He reached the building that blocked the tunnel from view. It remained as dark and empty as he remember and thank heaven for that. He waited until a few passing dwarves had moved on and hurried around behind it.

He found the tunnel unchanged and unguarded. Now if only his luck held a little longer.

Samaritan forced himself through the opening and down the narrow passage. He wanted to shout for Grub, but feared drawing attention. Just because the area around the tunnel had been empty when he arrived didn't mean it remained that way.

With a final grunt of effort he pulled himself out and into the modest cavern. Steeling himself, he released the illusion and activated his darkvision spell. No sign of Grub. In fact, he saw no sign of anything. No note or other hint of where he might find his guide. Samaritan doubted Grub got captured. With his magic and knowledge of the area, Grub would have little trouble evading a patrol.

No, it seemed he'd simply done what he promised and left after five days.

Frustrating as it was, Samaritan couldn't get angry at the dwarf. Grub hadn't lost track of time after all, he had. Now Samaritan had to figure out how to find the burial site on his own.

"You're late, human." Grub strode into the cavern from deeper down the tunnel. He carried a fat rat half as long as he was tall.

"I thought you'd left," Samaritan said, trying, and he feared failing, to keep his relief from showing.

"Decided to give you one more day. But I ran out of food." He held the rat up for closer inspection. "Had to go hunting. Did you get what you needed?"

"I think so, but I won't know for sure until we check. Are you familiar with a mass grave where the Black Iron Empire buried a number of murdered slaves?"

"Every dwarf knows that spot and if you mean to disturb it, I'll leave you here to rot." Grub held out his white cloak like it was a dirty thing.

Samaritan tossed the brown one aside and put it on. Having the familiar cloak around his shoulders felt right. "I have no intention of disturbing your dead. They were killed between two and three days' march from the site where they hid the giant beast. At least according to the historical account I read. I'm hoping the grave will be close enough for us to pick up some trace of the creature's corruption so we can follow it to our destination."

Grub grunted, seeming satisfied as long as Samaritan had no intention of desecrating the gravesite. Not that he would have hesitated to desecrate every grave between here and Tiber if that's what it took to find the beast.

While his guide got busy processing the rat, Samaritan slumped against the wall, closed his eyes, and ended all his spells. His entire body tingled with released tension. He'd failed to realize just how much being constantly on guard had cost him physically and mentally.

"You look worse than this rat," Grub said.

"Infiltration missions all take a toll. Give me an hour or two of rest and I'll be fine."

Grub snorted again and Samaritan didn't blame him. The lie sounded weak in his own mind. He knew better than anyone that he would never be truly well ever again.

Samaritan's rest lasted only half an hour then they were on the move. Thankfully, Grub led him to a bright cave only a couple hours' walk from the end of the tunnel. Using his magic, Grub heated a stone and set to cooking the rat meat. Samaritan's mouth watered. While he doubted roasted rat would compare favorably to the meal he enjoyed with Titus, he hadn't eaten anything fresh since entering the archive, so anything hot would be welcome.

"What else did you learn during your search?" Grub flipped the sizzling meat over and sprinkled some spice from his pack on it.

"I learned that your people had an exceedingly difficult time two generations ago. I didn't do an in-depth study, but apparently the geomancers were less than effective against the wizards of the Black Iron Empire. The powers that be welcoming the Tiberian Empire makes a lot more sense now."

Grub skewered a piece of meat and handed it to him, taking a second for himself. "The geomancers' failure at the Battle of Dwarfhome is our greatest regret. Our magic has been held in low regard ever since."

Samaritan found the grilled rat tasty enough. "You weren't

even born then. Why would your people hold current geomancers in contempt due to the actions of others?"

"It's less contempt for the geomancers themselves than it is for our style of magic. We specialize in finding our way through the tunnels, locating minerals, and stealth. The overwhelming might of the Black Iron Empire's demon-fueled sorcery rolled right over them. The battle didn't even deserve the name. The Slaughter of Dwarfhome would be more accurate."

They finished their meal in silence, Grub's sullen and Samaritan's thoughtful. He had a number of questions for his guide, but Samaritan forbore comment for now. What weighed most heavily on his mind was, after his fellow geomancers' failure to save Dwarfhome, why would Grub want to help destroy it again?

CHAPTER 16

Joran woke but didn't open his eyes. A slightly floral scent made him think he'd returned to his room in Alexandra's suite. Mia's warm, comfortable presence in the back of his mind reassured him that his soulmate had survived her encounter with the demon. What else might have happened and how long ago, he hadn't the least idea. The last thing he remembered was telling Mia not to give the sword back to Septimus. Having seen its properties, he knew they'd need it to deal with the many threats facing the empire.

"You can stop pretending, I know you're awake," Mia said.

Joran finally opened his eyes, pain free he noted with immense relief. He turned his head a fraction and found Mia smiling at him from one chair and Alexandra sound asleep in another. The silver sword leaned against Mia's chair in easy reach.

"Thank The One God, you kept it. How long have I been out?"

"Too long, but less long than I'd feared, about a day and a half. The pope nearly had a kitten when I refused to give him his precious sword and the emperor refused to order me to. Of course, I might not have given it back even if he had."

Joran sat up and found everything working right. He didn't try and see the ether. That particular test would keep until later. Someone had removed his robe, but he still wore the same underclothes.

"Hungry?" Mia asked.

"Starving. For future reference, if the emperor does give you an order, assuming it won't get us both instantly killed, you should obey. We could have recovered the sword some other way if it became necessary. We can't lose the emperor's support, not if we want to get to the bottom of the threat facing the empire."

Alexandra's soft chuckle drew their attention. "You two are the necessary ones, not Father, Marcus, or myself. The best thing we can do for the empire is support you and stay out of the way."

"You are necessary," Joran said. "Without your support, I would have collapsed long before we reached the vault. Thank you for that."

The Iron Princess actually blushed. Joran smiled then he smiled wider when Mia set a small table with a silver tray on it in front of him. Meat, bread, cheese, and fruit covered it and a jug of wine sat on the side.

"Won't you both join me?" Joran asked.

Alexandra stood and stretched. Joran finally noticed the bloodstain on her dress. His blood. She hadn't even changed since the fight.

"I need a bath and some clean clothes," Alexandra said. "Father sent someone to collect the church's books yesterday morning. They're in the lab."

"More reading. Great." She certainly knew how to kill the mood. "Thanks for staying with me."

"Where else would I be?" She waved and hurried out leaving Joran and Mia alone.

"She really has fallen in love with you," Mia said. "Do you think, soon…?"

Joran scrubbed a hand across his face. Good to see Mia's lust hadn't dimmed any. That more than anything convinced him that everything would be okay. For the time being at least.

"I think we're more apt to have to kill some other horrible monster before Alexandra and I end up in bed. She seems incredibly nervous about the whole thing."

He ate with a will and Mia picked around the corners. Soon enough the plate was empty.

When they'd finished, she asked, "What now?"

"Despite my lack of enthusiasm, I think we'd best head to the lab and take a look at the goodies the emperor brought. I sincerely hope Septimus sent everything. I'd be thrilled to never have to deal with a churchman again."

"Seconded."

Mia set the tray to one side and collected the silver sword while Joran hunted up a fresh robe. He didn't bother with a formal advisor's robe, settling instead for something a bit less stiff. He still had his platinum amulet for anyone that didn't recognize him. At this point, damn few people in the palace wouldn't.

They stepped out into the sitting room and found three of the servants waiting. They bowed as one.

"We're so glad you're okay, Lord Den Cade," Marsa said.

"I appreciate the sentiment, Marsa," Joran said. "Did you bring my snack?"

She nodded.

"It was delicious, thank you. If Alexandra's looking for me later, tell her we went to the lab to examine the books her father had delivered from the church."

"Of course, my lord." Marsa bowed again. "And please try to be more careful in the future."

Joran smiled. Somehow, he doubted that would be an option for the foreseeable future.

They left the suite and headed down the empty hall outside. When they'd gone a dozen strides Mia said, "I think Marsa might have a crush on you."

"I think she's afraid if I get myself killed, Alexandra will be impossible to live with. Besides, I'd never take advantage of a servant. It's too easy for noblemen. And even with the willing ones, you never know for sure if they're hoping for a bastard you'll have to support. Quintus did that once. Of course, Father's the one that ended up having to support her and the kid. I think he shipped them off to the western provinces somewhere."

They turned into the lab, drawing a nod from the guard on duty. He and his partners had strict instructions that only Joran, Mia, or a member of the imperial family had permission to enter.

Everything looked exactly as Joran left it save for a stack of twenty books newly added to the central workbench. A thick coat of dust covered them. Clearly the pope didn't spend a great deal of time reading the forbidden works. These looked dusty enough to have stayed untouched since the previous pope's time.

"They could have at least cleaned them." Mia ran a finger down the spine of one and held the filthy digit up for his inspection.

Joran nodded then shifted his gaze to the clean section of

spine. As soon as he read the text he grinned. This was the missing book he'd been wanting. It contained part of a detailed summary of the dwarves' time enslaved by the Black Iron Empire. An imperial researcher had done a complete outline of the dwarven archive when they joined the empire. Why the church felt the need to keep this particular volume he hadn't the slightest idea. Maybe it just got lost when they did the review and never made it to the Forbidden Section.

Then again, maybe it didn't.

Either way he had to make sure. Joran grabbed the book and settled into his reading chair. His eyes stung as if to complain about his treatment of them. As long as they didn't start bleeding again, he wouldn't worry.

"Anything I can do?" Mia asked.

"There's still lots of reading," he said.

"Maybe I'll go see if I can find a sheath for my new sword."

Joran grinned and turned back to his book. It seemed today wouldn't be the day he turned Mia into a researcher.

Over the years he'd done a lot of studying in the library and one of the most useful tricks he'd learned was how to quickly skim pages for the particular information he needed. In this case any mention of giant beasts, strange weapons, or corruption. He'd found enough hints in the volumes he'd already checked to know the Black Iron Empire did something in the dwarven territory, though the exact "what" remained a mystery.

The pages flew by, crinkling slightly and releasing occasional puffs of dust. Aside from two sneezes, Joran never looked away. He had no idea how long it took, but three-quarters of the way through the book he found what he needed. A one-sentence reference to the mass murder of a group of slaves. No one simply murdered perfectly useful slaves for no reason.

Unless those slaves knew something their masters wanted kept secret. Other hints scattered through various texts convinced Joran he'd found the clue he sought. Unfortunately, the researcher hadn't cared much about a group of dead slaves and Joran found no further information about the event.

If he wanted details, he'd have no choice but to travel north to Dwarfhome to explore the archive himself. With any luck, they'd have a librarian that could point him right to the information he needed.

He set the book in its place in the stack and headed for the door. No sign of Mia coming back. The armory probably didn't have a sheath that would fit her sword. Hopefully they had something close enough as he doubted they had time for a custom one to be made. Assuming Alexandra could arrange a dragon ship for him, Joran wanted to be on his way north today or tomorrow at the latest.

The short walk back to the suite took less than a minute and he slipped inside without knocking. The servant on duty smiled when he entered. The girls had relaxed around him which pleased Joran very well. The half-ancient slaves at home never seemed to relax no matter how nicely Joran treated them.

Alexandra's bedroom door opened and she leaned against the frame. She'd changed into a clean crimson robe and gold silk slippers.

"You look tired," Joran said.

"Yes, and it's all your fault. Don't worry me like that again." Her smile took the sting from her words.

"Do you have a minute?" he asked.

"I know that tone. You're planning something, probably

something dangerous. Do you have to go out again so soon?"

"I think I've got a line on the next giant beast. I'd like to try and get there before Samaritan can wake it. For the good of the empire, I'd prefer to keep the creature asleep. Even if we can kill it, The One God alone knows how much damage it might do to Dwarfhome before we do."

"It's near the dwarves?" He had her attention now. "That's the empire's wealthiest province. A catastrophe there would be a serious problem. They send us most of the high-quality steel we transform into imperial steel. We have other sources as well of course, but it would be a serious blow to the legions."

She started pacing, Alexandra having been replaced with the Iron Princess. He sensed Mia approaching and she seemed pleased. Maybe she'd found a sheath that fit after all. After the fight, she deserved a reward.

Alexandra turned to face him just as Mia stepped through the door. She had a new, black leather sheath belted on. The hilt of the silver sword and about half an inch of the ricasso didn't fit, but other than that everything looked good.

"I like it," Joran said.

Mia beamed. "The armorer said he'd never seen anything like the silver sword. I think he wanted to keep it, but I knew you wanted to get going."

"And even if I didn't, you should never let that weapon out of your reach. It might be the only way we have to defeat our enemies."

Alexandra cleared her throat and when Joran looked her way he winced. She wore a frown and had her hands on her hips.

"Sorry. You were going to say something?"

"I was going to say, the problem with traveling to Dwarfhome right now is the weather. That far north and in the mountains, snowstorms, some of them fierce, can be a serious problem. Under normal circumstances, I wouldn't even consider sending out a dragon ship until spring."

Joran didn't like the sound of that. On the other hand, did they really have a choice? "How does it compare to the danger of a giant beast attacking Dwarfhome?"

"In the grand scheme of things, it doesn't. The problem is, I don't care about anyone in Dwarfhome. You, however, I care about very much. The idea of you dying in a dragon ship crash makes my stomach twist." Alexandra moved closer and put her head on his chest. "I feared I might lose you in the vault. I don't want you to survive that only to die a few days later."

Joran stroked her hair. He loved the feel of it, the scent, everything.

After a moment he said, "I'm not overly eager to die myself, especially when I have so much to live for. However, I do have someone I care about in Dwarfhome. My brother Titus is there negotiating with the dwarves. Even without all the other issues, I would still have to try and warn him."

He stepped back and brushed a tear off her cheek. "So what do you say? Can I get a ship?"

Alexandra blew out a long sigh. "Of course. We both have our duty to perform, preferences be damned. It will be ready for you in the morning. I guarantee only vetted personnel will work on it. If anything takes it down, it won't be sabotage."

"I can ask for no more than that. And don't worry, we'll be back before you know it." He tried to sound reassuring, but Alexandra knew as well as he did just how serious a danger he and Mia faced.

Hopefully, having his soulmate at his side and a beautiful bride-to-be waiting for him, Joran would be able to keep his promise.

CHAPTER 17

Samaritan set a brutal pace through the tunnels and Grub showed no signs of faltering. If anything, the dwarf handled the double-time march better than Samaritan did. He'd never seen the dwarf sweat or even breathe hard from physical activity. Only excess magic laid him low. The stone around them seemed soft compared to Grub.

"We're getting close," Grub whispered.

Samaritan had no idea how he could tell one section of blank stone from another. Even when he peeked into the ether, he saw nothing that indicated that this part of the underground was any different from any other part of it. Maybe a geomancer saw things a regular wizard didn't. Not that Samaritan's few lessons entitled him to that name. Might be just a dwarf thing too. He really had no idea.

His thoughts were interrupted when Grub grabbed him by the front of the tunic and dragged him into an alcove barely deep enough to hold both of them. The smell of up-close dwarf made him frown.

"What—"

Grub clamped a sweaty hand over his mouth. The ether shimmered as an illusion covered the alcove entrance.

A moment later the thud of marching boots reached him. Several minutes passed before a group of twenty heavily armed and armored dwarves came stomping past. To a man they glowered around at everything.

One of them looked Samaritan dead in the eye. Long seconds passed then they were gone. Grub waited a good half a minute more before ending his spell and moving out into the tunnel.

"For a moment there I feared you'd lost your mind." Samaritan wiped the dwarf's sweat off his face. "Are there usually patrols in this area?"

"No. We've never heard about patrols around the memorial. It's just a steel plaque set into the stone with a few words about the fallen. There's nothing of value for anyone to steal."

"Then why the patrol?"

Grub shook his shaggy head. "I don't know and that worries me. Let's see if we can get close enough to look around. No talking and try not to walk so loudly."

How did anyone walk quietly on stone with heavy leather boots? His answer came a moment later when Grub started out again, this time making no more noise than a ranger in the forest. No ether swirled around the dwarf's feet, so this had to be something he'd learned from his people.

Samaritan did his best to imitate the way Grub stepped. Even so, his footfalls sounded horribly loud in his ears. Hopefully his nerves made the noise seem worse than it really was.

By some miracle they reached a side passage that offered a good view of the memorial. The sight did nothing to reassure him. A quick glance confirmed a full century of dwarf infantry.

The soldiers wore heavy mail and carried imperial steel axes. Every one of them looked grim and focused.

Grub tugged his cloak and they eased back the way they'd come. They went a full hundred yards before Grub said, "This isn't some random patrol. It looks like they're setting up a semipermanent camp. That means at least two more centuries are in the area. The only reason I can think of for a deployment of this scale is that they're looking for you."

Samaritan frowned. Only Titus knew he was in the area and even his dear friend had no idea where he intended to go next. In fact, he and Grub alone knew their destination and the dwarf seemed as surprised as he did to find soldiers here.

No, this had to be something else.

"Anything's possible, but how they know I'm here is the real mystery. But it really doesn't matter. We don't need to get to the gravesite, we only need to search the area for signs of corruption we can follow. A task, I grant, that has become a good deal more difficult with a few hundred soldiers patrolling the area. Did you see anything from our hiding place?"

"No. Did you?"

Samaritan shook his head. He'd come to trust the dwarf's sight more than his own. Geomancers appeared to be more sensitive to that sort of thing than the average wizard. Not that he came close to even being average at wielding the ether.

"What do you want to do?" Grub asked.

Talk about a difficult question. "The soldiers' presence changes nothing beyond increasing the difficulty of our task. Somewhere, within a few days' march, the beast is hidden. You know these tunnels far better than I do. If you were marching a column of slaves to Dwarfhome and this was about your halfway point, where would you have started from?"

Deep grooves formed in Grub's forehead as he thought. "This passage runs generally north and south, but it's one of the main tunnels and many smaller ones connect to it. Your beast is likely either due north, northeast, or northwest. I suppose we'll have to search them all, while evading soldiers, until we find it."

"We can certainly bypass the main tunnel. The imperial wizards wouldn't have hidden the beast where some random wandering wizard might notice it. It will likely be hidden down some seldom-used side tunnel."

"That narrows it down a bit, but there are still a lot of side tunnels. Where should we start?"

Samaritan shook his head. "You decide. Once we get anywhere close, the corruption should be easy to see. And by close I mean a mile or so. We may come across faint signs sooner than that, but I wouldn't count on it."

"Okay. Our best bet will be to swing well wide of the grave-yard and more importantly the soldiers guarding it, and start our search three days or so north of here working back toward Dwarfhome. That's a lot of territory to cover. Are you certain there's nothing else that might narrow it down further?"

Samaritan racked his brain, trying to figure out from what he'd learned in the archive and the serpent's hiding place where the second beast most likely slept.

He opened his mouth and Grub gave a shake of his head. The rhythmic thump of boots reached him a moment later. An illusion shimmered into place just before another patrol of ten soldiers went stomping past their hiding place. One of these times Grub would fail to get the magic in place quickly enough and they'd be in real trouble.

When the patrol had disappeared up the tunnel Samaritan said, "It's not the tunnels we need to search, but the caverns connected to them. If this beast is anywhere close to the same size as the serpent, we'll need a cavern at least fifty paces across and probably close to that high."

Grub closed his eyes and gave a resigned shake of his head. "Why didn't you say that in the first place? There can't be more than half a dozen caverns that size. I can find them easily with my magic. Let's get out of here before any more soldiers show up."

Samaritan followed Grub quickly and quietly away from their hiding place. For the first time since he began the search, he felt confident they might actually find what they sought.

CHAPTER 18

A mixture of howling wind, driving snow, and low clouds made the dragon ship flight even more harrowing than Joran expected and his expectations had been pretty low. He clutched the arm of his couch on the bridge and looked everywhere but out the window. He'd thought he'd overcome his fear of flying, but it seemed a blizzard brought it roaring back.

Mia sat beside him seeming perfectly at ease. Through their link he could tell she wasn't even faking. He envied her that courage.

Over the last few months, he'd faced down some horrible things and every time his knees shook and every instinct screamed at him to run. He didn't, or at least so far he hadn't. Every time, he wondered if this would be the time his nerve broke. Only Mia's steady presence combined with the knowledge of what might happen if he failed held him on course.

A particularly powerful gust slammed them to the right.

The ship's captain shot Joran a glare as if the storm was his fault. Or maybe he blamed Joran for having to fly north at this time of year. That, unfortunately, he had to accept the blame for.

"None of this is your fault," Mia said. "Stop thinking it is. That lunatic Samaritan caused all this trouble. If he'd just fall off a cliff somewhere, we could stay home and relax like normal people."

Joran smiled and patted her hand. "That's a lovely thought. A week in my lab with no one trying to kill me sounds like heaven. You, I fear, would be bored out of your mind."

"As long as no demons, giant beasts, or inquisitors showed up, I'd live with a little boredom. Not to mention a little peace would give you and Alexandra a chance to get better acquainted."

Her lust rushed through him, forcing Joran to roll his eyes. Even fighting a demon did nothing to lessen her desire for Alexandra. A perfectly reasonable feeling given the princess's beauty.

"The Dwarfhome hangar is in sight," the lookout said.

"Thank The One God," Joran muttered out of habit.

Something slammed into the ship.

They lurched left this time and started to fall.

A muffled voice emerged from one of the speaking tubes.

"Best brace yourselves, my lords," the captain said. "I don't know what hit us, but the balloon is losing gas. It's going to be a rough landing even if we make it to the runway."

Joran liked the sound of that not in the least. On the plus side, he had already tensed so much he doubted he could brace himself any harder. Given his total lack of control, he clamped his eyes shut and hoped for the best.

The shudders and rattles seemed worse with his eyes closed, so he quickly opened them again. Just in time to see the ground rushing up at them with alarming haste.

The impact knocked him off the couch despite being ready for it.

When the world stopped moving, he tried to stand. The angle of the deck made that a tricky prospect, but he managed after a couple false starts. Mia had already stood up a few feet away and the bridge crew wasn't far behind. Snow filled both the window and the floor viewport. They must be buried, at least partially.

"Did we miss the runway by much?" Joran asked.

The captain wobbled and grabbed a bent speaking tube. "I don't think so, Lord Den Cade. Perhaps a hundred yards at most."

A hundred yards was still a hell of a ways in this weather.

"Let's see if we can get to our gear and find a way out of here."

Mia took his hand and together they inched their way toward the exit. The forty-five-degree pitch of the deck made that no easy task. Fortunately, Mia's excellent physical skills made the difference and soon enough they were on their way to the second floor.

A quick stop at their room to collect his kit and their alchemically treated cloaks. The dark, heavy cloaks had properties similar to a White Knight's cloak. Joran created them a couple years ago, but the cost of the treatments made them too expensive for anyone to buy. His disgusted father said to just keep them. He'd never been anywhere cold enough to need them, but suspected they'd be glad to have them today.

Three crewmen loaded with tools hurried past them. Mia grabbed one and asked, "What happened?"

"Can't tell from inside," he said. "The balloon crew said they heard something hit before we started going down."

Mia released him and looked at Joran. "What do you think?"

"Nothing natural did this. The wind might push us around and the snow make us heavier, but neither of those things could bring down a dragon ship. If I didn't know better, I'd say a catapult stone or something similar hit us. Given that we're in the middle of snow-cloaked mountains supposedly controlled by our allies, that seems unlikely. Not that it matters for the moment. We still need to get out of here and into the city."

Never particularly athletic, it ended up taking Joran most of fifteen minutes to make the short trip to the lowest deck exit even with Mia's help. They found two crewmen trying their best to pound the hatch open with wooden sledgehammers. Even from a safe distance Joran could see that the frame had twisted just enough to bind the ramp.

"Can I persuade you to help those unfortunate fellows?" Joran asked.

"How can I help them?"

He tapped her sheathed sword. "If this cuts anything like the black one, it'll make short work of the ramp."

"I can try, I guess." She drew the sword and gave it an experimental swing as if that would give her a hint of how well it might cut.

"Hey, guys, give the lady some space," Joran said.

The crewmen finally noticed Mia standing there with a bare sword and hastened to get out of her way.

She stepped up to the hatch and with careful precision sliced three thin strips off the edges of the ramp. When she'd returned to Joran's side the men hurried back and easily shoved the hatch open. As soon as they did, a bitter wind blew in. The cloaks' magic rendered the wind just uncomfortable rather than unbearable.

They didn't have a chance to climb out before a bearded face appeared in the opening. "Is everyone all right?"

"As far as we know," Joran said. "Are you part of the rescue team? Our ship has taken considerable damage. It felt like a catapult stone hit us."

"You won't find a catapult within five hundred miles of here," the dwarf said. "More likely a rebel geomancer took a shot at you. The sons of whores pop up like gophers and disappear again just as fast. Who might I have the pleasure of addressing?"

"I'm Joran Den Cade and this is my sister, Mia. I believe His Imperial Majesty sent a message telling you to expect us."

"Lord Den Cade, welcome. We assumed this was your ship. Glad to see you're unharmed." The dwarf turned his head. "Bring up the ladder."

A minute later a pair of burly dwarves lowered a ladder to them and despite the awkward angle even Joran managed the climb out with minimal difficulty. Just as he guessed, they'd ended up in a snowy flat area about a hundred yards from the landing field. More groups were hurrying this way, carrying all manner of equipment.

The three dwarves that had helped them out all wore mail shirts, conical helms and had axes slung at their belts. Their crimson cloaks stood out almost painfully against the snow.

Speaking of cloaks, a gust of frigid wind made Joran extra glad he'd brought the enchanted cloaks for him and Mia. If the cold troubled the dwarves, they showed no sign of it. Considering how long they'd lived in this part of the world, perhaps they'd gotten used to the chill.

"We've made a path, my lord," the first dwarf they saw said.

"If you'll follow me, Governor Bramrule is eager to welcome you."

"Thank you, um..."

"Centurion Stoneheart of the First Dwarfhome Legion, my lord, at your service."

"Excellent, Stoneheart. I've never met a centurion I wouldn't trust with my life. I'm sure you'll be another fine example of your rank."

The dwarf drew himself up to his full if still modest height and looked Joran right in the naval. "I'm your man, Lord Den Cade."

"Lead on then," Joran said. "I'm sure the governor has a lot to tell me."

Stoneheart led Joran and Mia down a packed path toward the landing zone. More workers carrying tools Joran didn't recognize slogged past them toward the dragon ship. Hopefully everything he'd heard about the ingenuity of the dwarves turned out to be the truth. Just getting the downed dragon ship into a hangar looked like a monumental task.

Barring a miracle, they wouldn't be returning to Tiber before spring.

CHAPTER 19

It took most of half an hour to make the walk to the government compound through the underground city of Dwarfhome. Aside from sitting in the biggest cavern Joran had ever imagined, it looked like any other city. Two- and three-story stone buildings dominated the area with the occasional taller tower. They passed every kind of business you might find on the surface including a butcher shop with live animals in the back. Alchemical lights so big an adult could easily stand up inside the glass enclosure sat atop tall poles and lit the cavern.

Stoneheart and his two companions led them to a sprawling compound surrounded by a stone wall with a steel portcullis protecting the only entrance. Ten dwarves dressed much like Stoneheart stood with hands near their axes as the group approached.

Stoneheart moved a little bit ahead of them and announced, "Lord Den Cade to see Governor Bramrule."

The guards all offered smart salutes. A dwarf with a small silver hammer on his uniform said, "This is our week for

Den Cades. Your family must get along well with the governor."

Joran frowned. "Titus was here. Why?"

"He brought a scholar to visit the archive. I had no idea merchant houses sponsored scholarly research. I guess having 'sponsored by the Den Cade family' inside the cover must get your name out there."

Joran's frown deepened. Father had never sponsored anything that didn't offer a return and certainly no vague scholarly research. What the hell was Titus up to?

He shook his head. His brother would have to wait. All his focus had to be on finding the hidden giant beast before Samaritan showed up.

The portcullis clanked up and Stoneheart led them through and toward the governor's mansion. The two-story fortress mansion followed the standard imperial design with public rooms on the first floor and living quarters on the second. They passed between what Joran assumed were servants if the aprons and lack of armor were any indication. Three on each side of the main hall bowed as one as they passed. It seemed the governor wanted to make a good impression.

That worried Joran. Usually, if an imperial official had done good work, he felt no need to show off. Only the screwups tried to cover it up with pomp and showing off. Hopefully he misjudged the governor. If so, he would be pleasantly surprised.

Their walk ended in front of a door which Stoneheart knocked on.

"Come in," a muffled voice said.

Stoneheart opened the door and bowed. "I'll be waiting to guide you to your rooms, my lord."

Joran nodded his thanks and Mia followed him into a well-appointed office. All the furniture save the extra-high chair behind the desk was sized for humans. Strange. How many humans actually visited the governor of Dwarfhome?

Not many, Joran guessed. Whoever built this room probably did so with the idea of making sure the governor never forgot his place as a provincial. Exactly the sort of petty nonsense he'd expect from an imperial noble.

From behind the desk stepped the fattest dwarf Joran had ever seen. Streaks of gray ran through his beard. He dressed in fine crimson robes cut in the imperial style only shorter.

"Lord Den Cade, welcome." The governor reached out and gave Joran's hand an enthusiastic pump. "It's an honor to have you as our guest. And please allow me to extend my most enthusiastic congratulations on your upcoming wedding. Was your flight comfortable?"

"A bit rough but fine up until we got smashed out of the air. Centurion Stoneheart suggested rebel geomancers were involved. I didn't realize this province had such an active rebel presence."

Governor Bramrule winced. "There aren't that many of them, really. It just seems that they choose the worst possible time to lash out. We keep them largely isolated in the northern and eastern tunnels. We haven't had any issues with ore output or gem extraction."

"Maybe not," Mia chimed in. "But getting dragon ships knocked out of the sky is a serious problem. We got lucky that no one was hurt, but next time we might not be so fortunate."

"There won't be a next time." The governor ushered them into the chairs in front of his desk. When they'd settled in he continued. "I intend to make sure the area where dragon ships approach Dwarfhome is constantly patrolled. Had you come earlier in the season, they would have been patrolled and no enemy caster would have dared strike. It's just no one ever comes to visit this time of year."

He added that last in a voice that pled for understanding. Joran understood perfectly well that his ship got smashed out of the sky because this idiot didn't want to send out late autumn patrols. He gave a mental shake of his head. That thought sounded distinctly like Alexandra.

"We understand of course and we'll be sure to let the emperor know that you're doing your best, that no further attacks will be forthcoming, and that you'll cover all the expense of repairing our dragon ship."

That drew an enthusiastic nod. "Rest assured, my lord, that when spring arrives, your ship will be fully refit and ready to fly."

Joran would believe that when he saw it, but for now they had more pressing matters to discuss. "I assume you've deployed the legion as instructed."

"Of course. As soon as the message arrived, they departed for the memorial. We have the area fully under our control and patrols are expanding outward every hour. If this Samaritan is in the area, rest assured we will find him. I assume you wish him alive."

"We have no preference, Governor. As long as he's neutralized, alive or dead interests me not in the least."

"That makes it easier then. Would you like to speak with the generals? They're all at your disposal, ready to provide an hour-by-hour update."

"How many legions does Dwarfhome have?" Mia asked.

"Just one."

"Then why do you have multiple generals?" She cocked her head as if trying to understand. "Doesn't that muddle the chain of command?"

"Well, I like to reward certain people with a high rank when they do a good service for Dwarfhome. Most of them are generals in name only. They have no operational authority."

The more Joran heard, the less he liked the state of things in this province. Clearly someone should have spared the dwarves more attention. Just because the area stayed mostly peaceful didn't mean the government was functioning well.

"Find them new titles," Joran said in his seldom-used angry-noble tone. "A legion has one general so make damn sure it's the one that has some idea what he's doing. I'll be taking Centurion Stoneheart as my aide during my stay and his century can serve as my bodyguards. I intend to do some research in the archive to try and nail down exactly where the beast is hidden. When I get back, I expect a full report on the state of the search for Samaritan. Do I make myself clear?"

"Perfectly, Lord Den Cade. Rest assured everything will be ready when you get back. But please, wouldn't you rather have a higher-ranking aide than a mere centurion?"

"Stoneheart appears capable and that matters more than anything. Something to keep in mind as you make organizational decisions going forward. I expect good news when I return."

So saying Joran stood and stalked out the door. He found Stoneheart waiting a few strides up the hall.

The centurion snapped to attention. "Orders, Lord Den Cade?"

"You've been assigned as my aide and your century will serve as my guards until I leave. We're on our way to the archive. Lead the way."

Stoneheart quick-marched in front of him while the other two dwarves fell in behind. As they made their way through the hall toward the exit Stoneheart said, "The thing is, Lord

Den Cade, my century are the ones overseeing the rescue of the dragon ship's crew. The engineers are fine men for making repairs, but they're not so good at search and rescue."

"Not a problem," Joran said. "I don't intend to go out into the tunnels until tomorrow. That should give you plenty of time to finish the rescue operation and get them ready to march."

"A full day will be perfect. Thank you, my lord."

They emerged from the mansion and made their way toward the neighboring structure. The squat, square building didn't look like much compared to the imperial library. With any luck they could find what they needed quickly.

"You were kind of hard on the governor," Mia said as they walked. "I'm not sure I've ever seen you that upset."

"There are hundreds, probably thousands, of lives on the line and we have an at best marginally competent politician in charge of the response. I need him to understand that I will except nothing but the best and no sweet talk or bribe will get him out of trouble if he screws up. For The One God's sake you said it yourself. A legion has one general; the best one. It's not a title you hand out for kickbacks."

Stoneheart opened the door to the archive. "Here we are, my lord."

"Thank you." Joran stepped through and frowned. A bar ran the length of the room and behind it shelves of books were visible. Of a librarian he saw no sign. "Who's in charge of this place and where are they?"

Stoneheart climbed up on the bar and shook his head. "The librarian is resting."

Joran and Mia joined him and sure enough an unconscious dwarf lay beside a large bottle that stank of spirits.

"This is the librarian?" Joran asked.

"Unfortunately. Dak Bramrule is the governor's nephew. Suffice it to say he didn't get the job because he's overly qualified."

That might have been the biggest understatement Joran had ever heard. "If we wake him up, is there any chance he can tell us something useful?"

"I hesitate to say there's no chance," Stoneheart said. "However, there's no chance. If you wake him up now, he's more likely to vomit on your shoes than tell you where to find whatever information you're looking for."

Joran restrained a scream by the narrowest of margins. Assuming anything remained of Dwarfhome when the current crisis ended, he'd recommend the emperor replace the entire local government. Preferably by tossing every member of the Bramrule clan into the deepest crevasse in the mountains.

He looked to Stoneheart. "Is there any chance you can tell me where to find information about the Black Iron Empire? Specifically regarding the murder of a large number of slaves."

"Every dwarf knows the story of the great massacre. But if you want historical details, I fear I have little to offer."

"I understand. You're a soldier not a bloody librarian. We'll just have to look around. How do we get back into the archive?"

"There I can be of more help." Stoneheart reached over the bar and pressed something. A section of the bar swung out of the way and they stepped through.

The drunk librarian never flinched.

Row after row of shelves held hundreds of stone tablets. Okay, it was a library. There had to be a system of organization or no one would ever find anything. He just needed to figure out how the system worked.

"I see footprints," Mia said.

Joran squinted and just barely made out marks in the dust. They might have been anything, but he trusted Mia's enhanced senses far more than he did his own.

"Where do they lead?"

Mia walked down the rows before stopping about ten deep. "Right here. Looks like whoever came by took down everything from here to here."

She pointed at a section of tablets. Joran frowned and studied the spines. Based on the dates he figured they ran from the fall of the Black Iron Empire to a couple hundred years before. The latter matched the dates from the summary he read back in Tiber. Who in the world would have come here looking for the exact same information Joran wanted?

The answer made him a little sick. Only Samaritan would want that information.

Joran indicated the tablet farthest from the end of the empire. "Would someone take that down and put it on one of these ridiculously short tables please?"

Stoneheart beat Mia to the punch by a single step. While he wrestled the tablet off the shelf and over to the nearest table, Joran drank a translation potion. When he felt the magic settle in, he started reading.

The detailed version of events offered no more detail than the summary. It seemed the imperial wizards hadn't shared any information about why the slaves were killed or what they'd been doing out in the wild tunnels. Joran actually had a pretty good idea what they were doing, hiding the giant beast. Happily, if he couldn't find the information he needed, then Samaritan couldn't either.

The fallen White Knight would have to search the area around the memorial, moving away from Dwarfhome. The dwarven legion should be swarming through that area. If luck stood with them, they should run into Samaritan and either capture or kill him.

Given what he had to work with, Joran held out little hope.

"If I wanted to find out who had visited the archive in the past month or so, who would I speak to? Not the librarian, clearly."

"The guards at the main gate would know," Stoneheart said. "They keep track of everyone that enters or leaves the government compound."

"Splendid, put that tablet back and let's go talk to them." After what the gate guard said about his brother, Joran had a horrible feeling, but he refused to think about it until he had some actual proof that Titus betrayed the empire.

While Stoneheart returned the tablet, Joran turned to Mia. "Excellent work spotting those tracks. You probably saved us days of searching."

She smiled. "Anything that gets us out of the library quickly is a good thing in my book. You seem troubled."

"I'm worried about Titus. I fear he may be in trouble. Hopefully I'm just overly anxious and nothing will come of it."

"Your instincts haven't led us wrong yet and I doubt they will this time."

Joran shook his head. "In this case, I hope we're both wrong."

Stoneheart led them out of the archive. The unconscious librarian never stirred. Joran badly wanted to kick him, but he was probably so numb he wouldn't feel it.

The short walk to the main gate took only a minute. Joran let Stoneheart take the lead as they approached the gathered guards.

"Centurion," the chief guard said. "How can we be of service?"

"We need to know everyone that has visited the archive over the past month."

"That's easy enough," the guard said. "We've only had two. Titus Den Cade and the scholar in his employ. The governor gave orders that they were to have whatever access they needed. Lord Den Cade only stayed for an hour or so, but the scholar stayed in the archive for five days before leaving in a hurry. Is everything alright?"

Stoneheart looked to Joran for an answer.

"No, I fear everything is not alright. I know your century is otherwise occupied, but can you scrounge me up a dozen soldiers for a trip into the foreign merchants' quarter? I doubt there will be trouble, but better safe than sorry."

"I'll check the barracks," Stoneheart said. "Can I have ten minutes?"

Joran nodded and Stoneheart trotted off. A ten-minute reprieve before he'd have to confront his brother and find out if he was a traitor to the empire.

And if he was, The One God help them all.

CHAPTER 20

Samaritan hid behind a boulder beside Grub as yet another patrol marched past. Over the last two days he'd lost track of how many soldiers they'd seen. If it was fewer than a quarter of the legion he'd have been surprised. Despite the number of searchers, a combination of Grub's magic and knowledge of the area allowed them to remain hidden and check out ten potential caverns. Unfortunately, all ten showed no sign of corruption or any other sort of magic. They were just big, empty spaces.

Despite his devotion, if they didn't find something soon, he feared he might lose his mind.

When the sound of the soldiers' boots vanished in the distance, Grub motioned him up.

"This is getting absurd," Grub said. "What did they do, deploy the entire legion?"

"If they somehow found out about the beast, it's possible. Given the damage one of them could do, I can fully understand why they'd use whatever resources available to try and stop it from waking. Lucky for us, they seem to have no more idea where to find it than we do."

"I'm not sure how lucky we are, but we need to keep moving." Grub placed a hand on the wall and ether flowed out.

He immediately jerked his hand back.

"What is it?" Samaritan asked.

"A vein of corruption, as black as any I've ever encountered."

"That must be it. Can you trace it to the source?"

"*You* probably could." Grub's tone held a derisive note Samaritan didn't care for. "Look close."

Samaritan had been avoiding using the ether save when absolutely necessary to restore his always-weakening body. He should be rested enough now.

Shifting his vision, he looked closely at the tunnel wall. While he'd hardly call it a vein, a thin line of dark energy ran through the stone. Despite Grub's reassurances, Samaritan doubted he'd have noticed it if Grub hadn't pointed the corruption out. That just proved again how much more the dwarf had developed his sight. Perhaps the derision he'd shown had been deserved.

"I see it, but only barely. You'd best stay in the lead."

Grub shrugged and set out. He kept his hand just above the stone, a thin trickle of ether connecting him to it. Samaritan had never seen that particular technique. Of course, he'd seen so few it would have been a bigger surprise if he recognized the spell.

He blinked away the ether. For all his sight added to the job, he'd be better off saving his strength.

The pair followed the corrupt line for most of an hour without encountering another patrol. The soldiers had to be around here and he saw no magic of Grub's that might be hiding them. That being the case, why hadn't they encountered another patrol? He had no idea, but his gut instinct said they were running into something bad.

A faint sound reached him and after a moment Grub said, "I hear voices and they're right in our path."

Samaritan cursed. He knew it! Things had been going too smoothly.

"Can you tell what they're saying?"

Grub dropped to all fours and pressed his ear to the tunnel floor. Ether streamed out.

After a moment he said, "The centurion in charge says they found something important. He ordered a messenger dispatched to Dwarfhome. The rest of his century are forming a perimeter around the cavern."

The two of them against ninety-nine elite dwarven legionnaires weren't the sort of odds Samaritan liked. Taking them on would be an excellent way to end his quest in a hurry. They needed help, but first he had to confirm what the soldiers had found.

Time to use one of the spells that exhausted him the most.

Taking a deep breath, Samaritan extended his sight up and out of his body before sending it sailing down the tunnel toward the waiting soldiers. It took only seconds for him to spot the first legionnaire. The dwarf stood at the end of the tunnel, fully armed and armored in imperial steel. Fortunately, he showed no sign of noticing Samaritan's spell.

His invisible eyes continued on and a little deeper into a large cavern he spotted a ring of dwarves surrounding a round pool of Black Bile about fifty feet across.

He swallowed. That had to be the source of the corruption. Likely at the bottom he'd find the second beast.

Samaritan blinked his vision back to his body and sagged. Even such a short use of the spell wore him out.

"They beat us to the target," Samaritan said. "Will the other rebels help us seize the cavern so I can wake the beast?"

"Our cell isn't nearly big enough to drive off a full century of legionnaires. The whole reason we agreed to help you was so the beast could attack and destroy the traitors in Dwarfhome, not so we'd end up dead fighting the legion ourselves."

"If you're willing to put nothing on the line, then we might as well leave. Without access to the cavern, I can do no more."

Samaritan imagined he heard Grub's teeth grinding. "I can send a message and tell them we found the beast's hiding place. There are two other cells not that far from our camp. If they agree to help, there's a chance we can drive the legion out long enough for you to do whatever you need to. If reinforcements show up, we're done."

"Send your message. I'll contact the archbishop and see if she has the items I need to wake the beast. Assuming you don't know any soulbound pairs."

Grub shook his head. "I can't remember the last time dwarven soulmates were announced. Not in my generation certainly. We need to move somewhere before I start my spell. I can't send the message and shield us from detection."

They retreated to a narrow crack in the tunnel that Grub found with his magic. They forced their broad shoulders through and emerged in a chamber barely big enough for them both to sit down. Far from ideal, but given their circumstances it would serve.

Samaritan settled on the smooth stone and took out his amulet. Ether flowed and soon his thoughts were on their way to the archbishop. If she didn't have what he needed, Samaritan didn't know what he'd do next.

———

Given the fact that Fane essentially had forever to complete her mission, you'd think she'd be better at waiting. But you'd be wrong and if you were stupid enough to point this out, you'd also be dead in short order.

In an inner chamber of her citadel, she had an empty room that served only one purpose. It gave her a place to pace and think. She'd spent a lot of time here lately. Fane had no real reason to think time grew short if she wanted to complete her quest. But for some reason she'd had the nearly overwhelming feeling lately that if she didn't accomplish her goal soon, she never would.

At the moment she was waiting to hear from one of her cultists or Samaritan about the search for the second giant beast. Overseer was on his way to the site of corruption she spotted, but she doubted she'd hear anything from him for weeks since he had to travel at the speed of his human pawns.

For all its many strengths and abilities, at times like these she cursed her immortal body for its weakness to sunlight. It kept her trapped in her citadel when she really wanted to be out in the field. As always her master proved far wiser than Fane. He'd warned her that her choice of undead forms would be limiting, but her desire to retain her beauty along with gaining eternal life had blinded her to more practical options.

Now she had to deal with her situation.

The faint tingle of someone initiating contact brought a smile to her pale face only to have it vanish a moment later.

Naturally it would be the one person she had no real desire to hear from. "Yes, Beastmaster?"

"That guy you wanted me to keep alive, he's not doing so good. My pets get along fine with raw meat and not terribly fresh water, but he's really struggling. If you still want to keep him alive, I can arrange some better food for him, but humans just aren't tough enough to live in the maze for a long time. In another week or two, better food or not, he's going to be dead."

Fane ground her teeth. She did not need this right now. The White Knight probably knew nothing useful anyway. But if he did and she missed some tiny, vital clue that might make the difference in completing her task...

"Do you have somewhere else you can keep him? I'm in the middle of several projects at the moment."

Beastmaster's annoyance leaked through their connection despite his best effort to hide it from her. "I don't have a prison here, you know. I do research and make monsters, not babysit."

"I've seen your flesh pits. Throw him in one of those. You must have one you're not using. A little fresh straw and a heat stone should see him through long enough for me to finish up here and interview him." A fresh presence scratched at the back of her mind. "I have to go. Keep him alive for a little while longer."

Fane severed the connection before Beastmaster had a chance to offer any more excuses. Hopefully he'd do what she said. Punishing him wasn't something she'd try without a really good reason. Fane had no doubt she overmatched him in terms of raw power, but Beastmaster was easily the next strongest of her allies and a confrontation, even if she won, would leave her weakened in more ways than one.

She shook her head. It wouldn't come to that. For all his complaining and childlike tantrums, Beastmaster had never failed her and he wouldn't do so now. She turned her attention to the second person trying to reach her and let out a sigh of relief when she recognized Samaritan's presence.

"Tell me something good," Fane said.

"I'm pretty sure I found the second beast's hiding place, a giant pool of Black Bile. Anyway, I need a complete soul to sacrifice so it will wake. According to Grub, there are no soul-mates among the dwarves at the moment. Do you have one?"

In fact, Fane had captured three complete souls. They, along with her remaining black iron swords, were the rarest items in her collection. She wouldn't hand one over lightly.

"What do you have to offer in exchange?" she asked.

"What do you mean? I offer you the destruction of Dwarfhome and any imperials in the area. I've been doing all the legwork in this partnership. It's time for you to contribute something."

Fane disliked his attitude, but admired his spirit. So few people had the courage to speak with her like that. Actually no one living had done so in centuries. Even Beastmaster lacked the nerve.

She shook off the completely irrelevant thought and considered Samaritan's point. Having him running around causing trouble did serve her greater purpose by keeping those who might interfere with her true intentions too busy to do so. And really, despite their rarity, she had little use for the complete souls she'd collected. Gathering them had mainly been an experiment to see if it was possible.

"Very well, I'll send you one. Use it well, or you'll never see a second." Fane severed the link and left the empty room where she'd been pacing.

A short walk brought her to her workshop. All manner of books, equipment, and supplies covered half a dozen tables and shelves. Some might see a mess, but she knew exactly where everything rested and was able to make sure anything that might have a bad reaction stayed well away from her most valuable items.

Speaking of which, on the rearmost table sat a small black box. She lifted the lid, revealing three black pearls bigger than her thumb knuckle. Just looking at them made her smile as she remembered successfully extracting the souls of two people at once and merging them into one. Her master would have been proud of that feat. On the downside, the merged soul didn't allow her to extract the knowledge of either individual, rendering them virtually worthless beyond their monetary value.

Well, she'd get some value out of one of them now.

Fane grabbed the rightmost pearl, the one she'd had the longest. A touch of ether allowed her to sense the captured soul's wails of torment. Such sweet music. She stroked the pearl's slightly rough surface. Don't worry, you'll be free soon and in a great cause as well. Take pride in that and know your suffering has served a higher need.

The bound soul had no way of hearing her thoughts of course, but it pleased Fane to share them anyway. Spending her time alone, surrounded by enslaved undead, forced her to talk to herself from time to time. Some might have thought the centuries of isolation had driven her mad, but they were wrong. The lack of distractions helped her think more clearly, except when her allies felt the need to pester her.

Fane drew a circle in the air and filled it with ether. She pictured Samaritan, or more precisely his amulet, and commanded a micro portal the size of her hand to open. The ether shuddered and fought until she finally imposed her will on it. When the portal stabilized, she reached through and dropped the pearl in Samaritan's lap.

When Fane ended the spell a moment later her knees wobbled and she nearly collapsed. Even her undead body retained limits. Though that would all change when she found the dragon and mastered its power.

On that day, Fane would take her place among the mightiest wizards.

CHAPTER 21

The foreign merchants' quarter featured a number of fine hotels named after different precious metals. According to Father, Titus had a suite of rooms in The Golden Rest. Not that Joran needed to know the name. All he had to do was tell Stoneheart to guide them to the finest and therefore most expensive inn in the city. A Den Cade on a trade mission had a reputation to maintain and nothing less than the best would do.

Besides, grumble as Father might, the cost would barely be noted in the annual budget.

"Wow," Mia said. "It's just like Tiber at night only underground. Have you been here before?"

Joran grinned. "Before I went south, I'd never left Tiber. I've seen more of the world in the past few months than in my entire life previous. I've also seen enough property damage and death to last two lifetimes."

"Just ahead on your right, my lord," Stoneheart said.

The centurion had collected ten off-duty guards from the governor's barracks and added them to the two soldiers already with him. The guards hadn't seemed overly excited to spend their time off protecting a visiting noble, but Stoneheart had a way of persuading people to focus on the problem in front of them. At least Joran assumed he did. Aside from their scowls, the guards hadn't uttered a word of protest in his hearing.

The Golden Rest had a porch wrapped around it with chairs and wealthy-looking patrons sat chatting, drinking, smoking, and no doubt scheming about how best to take advantage of the person across from them. In short it served as a perfect example of the empire in miniature. He paused a moment to dig a detect-deception potion out of his kit and drink it down. Sad as it made him, he didn't dare leave figuring out the truth of Titus's answers to his own judgement. His family bias might make it hard for him.

When the potion had taken effect they climbed the stairs to the porch. Joran saw no one familiar among the staring faces. That suited him fine as he wanted to talk to his brother not fend off the attention of some noble he'd met years ago and whose name he'd long since forgotten. Given the nervous looks they shot the armed dwarves behind him, Joran figured no one even noticed him or Mia.

He doubted Samaritan was still in the area, but just in case he said, "Have the guards stay out here and detain anyone that tries to leave. I suspect the one we want is long gone, but better safe than sorry."

"Yes, Lord Den Cade." Stoneheart barked a few orders and the conscripted guards spread out around the inn. "Any other orders?"

"Not right now. Hopefully Titus is in his room and he can tell me everything I need to know."

Inside the common room twenty tables sat, neatly spaced

far enough apart to make it difficult for anyone to listen in on anyone else's conversation. His now-smaller entourage drew almost as many looks here as they did outside. What did those nervous glances mean? Which of these no-doubt-loyal merchants would sell out the empire for the right money?

Much as he hated to admit it, probably all of them.

Stoneheart led the way over to the bar where a fat dwarf—though not as fat as the governor—stood polishing a mug. He eyed them with distaste more than fear. Joran didn't care for that look, but also didn't care enough to say anything.

"Which room is Titus Den Cade's?" Stoneheart asked without preamble.

"I can't just give out information about a guest, especially a high-ranking noble one." The snotty reply came out in a surprisingly deep voice.

Stoneheart grabbed him by the apron and yanked him halfway across the bar. "There are times to be brave and times to obey. This is the latter. Much as I'd enjoy beating the information out of you, we're in a hurry. So I'll ask once more. Which room?"

The bartender rapidly went from arrogant to terrified. A perfect time for Joran to step in.

He placed a restraining hand on Stoneheart's shoulder. "I'm sure this good fellow is only doing as he was instructed. Rest assured, sir, my brother won't be upset if you tell us which room is his. My name is Joran Den Cade and I need to speak with him on a matter of some urgency."

"The owner told me never to give out a guest's information. I was just following orders. You understand?" That last came out in a pleading tone. Why anyone thought that would work on an imperial noble Joran had no idea.

"I understand completely. The room?"

"Number one, top of the stairs and turn right."

"Thank you." Joran offered a pleasant smile and led the group toward the stairs at the rear of the common room.

"I love watching you do that," Mia said. "You stepped in at the exact right moment."

"Centurion Stoneheart did the hard part. He played the tough guy. All I needed to do was offer a way out and the bartender jumped for it. Well done, by the way, Stoneheart."

"Thank you, my lord. Though I wasn't really pretending. I'd have happily beaten the information out of him. I have no use for snobs."

Joran chuckled. "Best keep that sentiment to yourself when dealing with the nobility. They're pretty much all snobs."

Stoneheart winced. "I meant no disrespect, Lord Den Cade."

"Oh, you didn't offend me. I know exactly what my peers are like and have about as much use for them as you do. I offered the warning as a sign of good faith. You seem like a good man and The One God knows Dwarfhome can use all of those it can get. I'd hate to see you offend someone and end up posted far away where you couldn't help."

At the top of the steps, they turned and soon found themselves standing in front of room number one. Joran took a deep breath to steady himself. Don't jump to conclusions. Titus might have a perfectly reasonable explanation for what happened at the archive.

He turned to Stoneheart. "You three wait out here. Mia and I will talk with my bother on our own. Make sure we're not disturbed."

"Yes, my lord." Stoneheart stepped back against the wall and motioned one of his men to either end of the hall.

"It'll be okay," Mia said. "I'm here for you whatever happens."

"Thanks. That means more than I can tell you."

Time to stop delaying. Joran knocked and a few seconds later the door opened. Titus's eyes widened when he saw Joran. "Little brother, this is a surprise. What brings you to Dwarfhome? Are Mother and Father okay?"

"They're fine and the rest is a long story. One best not told in the hall of a public inn."

"Of course, please forgive my poor manners. Come in."

Titus moved out of the doorway and they stepped into a sitting room every bit as nice as Alexandra's. Two leather chairs separated by a table sat in the center and Joran settled into one of them. Mia stayed standing behind him. Probably handier with a sword belted at her waist.

For his part Titus smoothed his gray robe, looked from Mia to Joran and back, smoothed his perfectly trimmed mustache, and finally sat in the second chair. Seeing his brother act so nervous only served to confirm Joran's worst suspicions. He'd never seen Titus this on edge.

"Aren't you going to introduce me to your friend?" Titus asked.

"Titus, this is Mia, my soulmate and our adopted sister."

Titus's jaw dropped. "Mother agreed to adopt a commoner into the family? I can't believe it."

"It came at the emperor's personal request," Mia said. "Joran's to marry Princess Alexandra in the spring."

Titus shook his head. "I'm very confused. I've only been gone since spring. How did all this happen?"

"As I said, it's a long story and it begins with a man that calls himself Samaritan." Titus flinched and Joran went on. "Do you know him?"

"No."

Joran scrubbed a hand across his face. And so the lies began. How he wished he'd been wrong.

"Try again, Titus."

"Did you take a lie-detection potion before coming up here? Don't you trust me?"

"Spare me the wounded innocent act, you're not as good at it as Quintus. Since you've already lied to me once, why would I trust you? What does this man have on you?"

Titus seemed to collapse in on himself and he leaned back in the chair. "Bellator has nothing on me. We're friends and we have been since our first year of college. He's revealed many of the empire's secrets since he came back from his quest to trace the Prophet's journey."

"I figured he attended imperial college and learned at least basic alchemy. If you two became friends, it means he's a noble of at least modest rank. What's his full name?"

Titus looked away and stayed silent.

"This isn't some childhood prank! Samaritan is responsible for the deaths of hundreds, and if he gets his way, he'll kill many thousands more. We have to know everything. If you won't tell me, you'll tell the Inquisition."

Titus's head snapped up. "You won't turn me over to those butchers. I know you, Joran. You hate them more than I do."

"I do hate them, but I swear on our family name, if you don't tell me everything right now, I'll watch them wring the truth out of you. I'll hate every minute of it, but there's too much on the line for half measures. If Samaritan finds the second giant beast and it comes for Dwarfhome, I can't even imagine how much damage it might do. My personal preferences mean nothing in the face of such a threat."

"The empire needs to die, Joran. It's evil. Once it's gone, we can build something better. Something fair and good. Bellator understands that and once I explain everything, you will too."

Titus believed he was telling the truth. Joran crossed his legs and rested his hands on his knee. "Make your pitch."

"Bellator and I met our first year of college as I said. There's no reason why we should have become friends, especially given our families."

"Who is he, Titus?"

Titus sighed. "Bellator Den March."

"As in Den March Trading, Father's biggest rival?" Joran stared, a few things finally falling into place. "You've been helping them. That's why they've been giving the family such fits lately."

Titus nodded. "I have. Even with my help they're really no threat to us. His parents were destroyed when they thought Bellator died. Their business would have fallen apart if I hadn't stepped in. I helped them out of a sense of mercy. But in the grand scheme of things that means nothing."

"I doubt Father would agree, but go on. Get to the part you think is important."

"About two years after Bellator left on his quest, I was out inspecting some of our trading posts near the border of the Land of the Blood Drinkers and who comes knocking on my inn door but the dear friend I thought was dead. In fact, he didn't look all that much better than a dead man. He had scars on his face and a gaunt, haunted look. The faithful, optimistic man I knew was dead. He went by Samaritan and he told me he planned to destroy the empire. I thought that was the stupidest thing I'd ever heard and told him so."

"Nice to see you retained some sense. Though where it's gone to now I can't imagine."

"You've got it backwards, Joran. Now I have sense. Now I

understand everything. The church sent people to kill him. They failed, but succeeded in killing his soulmate."

A little gasp from behind him confirmed Mia felt the same as Joran. Had someone sent killers after them and succeeded in taking Mia, Joran could well imagine his reaction would be the same as Bellator's. Unfortunately, as much as he understood how badly that would hurt, it changed nothing about what actually needed to happen. One man's pain didn't make the destruction of millions of people's way of life justified.

"I feel for him," Joran said. "I really do. And to be honest, if he wanted to spend his time killing churchmen, I probably wouldn't bat an eye. But a lot of innocent people died in Stello Province because of what he did. People who had nothing to do with the crime committed against him. You're okay with that?"

"It's unfortunate," Titus said. "But before you judge our intentions, you need to know the rest. The empire is built on a lie. The One God is a lie. The Prophet just made it up. The empire's primary reason for being, the spread of the faith, is built on a foundation of fiction."

"I know it's a lie." Joran grinned at his brother's slack-jawed reaction. "And it doesn't matter. Maybe four hundred years ago it would have. The empire is so much bigger and more vital than some stupid religious mandate. You can't be so blind that you can't see that. The primary problem in the empire right now is your cultist friends. Did Samaritan tell you a cell of them nearly killed your wife and sons along with Mother, Father, Mia, and I?"

"Are they all okay?" The desperation in Titus's voice gave Joran hope that his brother hadn't lost all reason.

"Yes, thanks to Quintus of all people. You've made a deal with murderers and lunatics, Titus. The new world you want to build is going to have a foundation of blood and bone. These people, Samaritan included, will kill tens of thousands of innocents if they have to. Will you? Because if you help them, the blood of those innocent people will be on your hands as well."

Titus slumped in his chair. "It all made so much sense when Bellator told me about the future the cult wanted to create. A fair place, without nobles or slaves. The provincials seem so pathetic when I travel the empire. So eager to please. I imagined them having more pride in themselves and their culture before we came and destroyed it. I just wanted to help give them back what we took."

How in The One God's name could such a hard-headed and talented merchant also be such a naive idiot?

"What are you going to do, Titus?"

Titus blew out a long breath and Joran would have sworn he saw a little of his brother's soul slip out with it. He reached under his tunic and pulled out a bronze amulet with a slashed red circle on the front. It looked just like the one they'd taken from the dead assassin.

"Bellator sometimes contacts me with this. He's going to send me a warning before he wakes the second beast. Take it. If you can't stop him, at least it will provide a warning to Dwarfhome."

Joran shook his head. "No, Titus. You're not going to dump your problems into my lap. We're going to speak with the governor. I'll tell him you've been working for me to gather information on the cult. If Samaritan contacts you, play along and let the governor know what's coming. Between the two of you, hopefully you can save the bulk of the people should Mia and I fail. It's time to join the fight, brother. On the right side this time."

"He's my friend, Joran. I think I might be the only one he has left. If I betray him, it might destroy his remaining humanity."

"You've seen what he's capable of. Do you want to be his friend or do you want to stop him from killing thousands of innocents? One or the other, Titus. If you refuse to help, I'll take the amulet and give it to the governor in the hope that Samaritan can't tell who's on the other end. I'll also have you placed under house arrest in the governor's mansion. One way or the other, your days of aiding that traitor are over."

Titus shook his head and loosed a bitter chuckle. "When did you get so tough? Last I saw you, all you cared about was your work. Now you act like you're some kind of hero of the empire."

"I'm not a hero, I'm a citizen. All citizens, but especially a pureblood noble like you or me, owe everything we have to the empire. If it falls, the provincials and everyone we haven't invaded yet will hunt us down and slaughter us. Mother, Father, Camellia, the boys, all of us. We are the empire, Titus. If it falls, so do we."

"Okay, I'll meet you at the governor's mansion in the morning."

The lie made Joran's stomach ache. "No, Titus. We're going now. Pack your stuff."

Titus looked left and right, like a trapped animal seeking escape. "I can't just pack up and leave. I have messages to write. There are meetings scheduled. If I just go, it will look bad for Den Cade Trading."

More lies. For all his talk, Titus had no intention of helping. The thought sickened Joran, but the truth was the truth. His brother had turned traitor, a blind, idiot, true believer in The One True God cult.

"Stop. I drank a detect-deception potion before I arrived. Your lies sicken me, Titus. I'm embarrassed to admit that I always considered Quintus the black sheep of the family, but for all his flaws, when the bell sounded, he fought for his family. Take the amulet off and hand it to me, slowly. I'm sure the governor can find a comfortable room with the lock on the outside for you to use for the rest of your time in Dwarfhome."

Titus slumped and dropped his hands to his lap.

A moment later he looked up, his eyes wide and insane.

He pulled a knife from somewhere and lunged at Joran.

Titus made it halfway across the table before Mia's silver sword lashed out, cutting the knife blade off at the handle.

A stiff blow from the pommel put him down for the count.

Mia looked at Joran. "I'm sorry. I know you didn't want it to go this way."

"No, I didn't, but from the moment I heard about the 'scholar' I feared it would. Titus always seemed like the most reliable and together member of the family. How am I supposed to tell Mother and Father?"

"I have no answers," Mia said. "But I promise I'll be there with you when you do."

Joran took her hand and gave it a squeeze. Her support meant the world to him. If he'd had to do this on his own, he feared his will might have broken. Not to mention Titus's knife would likely have spilled his guts all over the fine hardwood floor.

"Let's get him out of here while he's unconscious. If anyone asks, we'll tell them he's sick and going to the mansion for treatment. That should keep the damage to a minimum."

Joran collected the amulet while Mia called in Stoneheart and his men. His life kept getting harder and more complicated and he shuddered to think what might happen next.

CHAPTER 22

Samaritan didn't believe his luck. For so long it seemed everything had gone against him. But whatever Grub said must have been the right thing, because only a couple days after the message went out not only did the forty or so dwarves of Grub's cell show up, but another hundred from two others as well as a pair of geomancers.

The two magic users were an unexpected bonus and should make what they had to do much easier. They'd gathered in one of the large, empty caverns Samaritan and Grub had checked earlier in hopes of finding the sleeping beast. The geomancers had done something to keep the patrols from stumbling into them.

The leaders of the three cells had their heads together trying to figure out their plan of attack. Samaritan would have no part in the planning. That had been made clear to him from the moment they arrived. And he didn't mind. He had other matters that required his focus.

He rubbed the black pearl and shuddered as he remembered the archbishop's pale hand appearing out of nowhere to drop it in his lap. The power that surged through the ether from her spell left him shaking. Samaritan had known her power made his own look like a candle beside a torch, but until that moment hadn't fully grasped exactly what that meant.

He understood now. Understood that should he ever do anything to stand in her way, the resulting battle would last slightly less than the blink of an eye and he would be on his way to join his soulmate in whatever afterlife awaited them.

A sigh nearly escaped him. Would that really be so bad? They hadn't been together for that long, but he missed her so much. He felt broken and understood he would until death claimed him. Everyone knew the downside of finding your soulmate, and even so he wouldn't have traded their time together for anything.

The pearl went back into a hidden pocket of his cloak and Samaritan stood. The leaders needed to make up their minds soon. The moment someone in charge figured out how important that bile pool was, they'd have the entire legion between them and it.

"You look anxious, human," Grub said.

Samaritan had been so focused on the gathering across the cavern he hadn't even noticed his guide approaching. "It's hard not to be since all our efforts will come to nothing if their strategy fails. It seems my fate always depends on the actions of others. It's not a pleasant feeling."

Grub shrugged, seeming indifferent to his concern. "When you work alone, that's unavoidable. Looks like they're done."

He turned back and sure enough the gathering had broken up. All the rebels moved toward the center of the cavern where the leaders waited to speak with them. Samaritan and Grub stood at the outer edge of the gathering. A part of and yet separate from the others.

Samaritan knew why he stayed apart. He was an outsider. Once he had completed his mission, whatever happened here interested him not in the least beyond his desire to see as many imperials as possible die.

But Grub's seeming reluctance to join the others of his cell struck him as strange. When one of the rebel leaders started to speak, he dismissed the matter as not his concern.

"We've settled on our plan of attack," the dwarf said. Samaritan didn't know him, but unless he was mistaken, the dwarf led the largest cell. "Since there's only one entrance to the target cavern, we'll attack in waves, twenty at a time, until we grind the imperial dogs down to a bloody pulp."

The rebels thrust their fists into the air, brandishing a motley assortment of weapons, none of which looked like imperial steel. At least they had sense enough not to cheer. That much noise would be heard regardless of the precautions taken.

"A lot of people are going to die today," Grub said. "I hope you can make good on your promise."

Samaritan hoped he could as well. The twin lizardmen had been willing sacrifices, making his task far easier. Calling forth the complete soul from the black pearl was probably beyond his meager skill. He hoped that by dropping the pearl into the bile pool, the beast would sense the offering and wake to consume it. Assuming that was how the magic actually worked. He hadn't the slightest idea how such advanced spells functioned.

"I hope so too. If I fail, I'll end up just as dead as the rest of you."

While not technically true since he always had his emergency escape spell, if he did fail, the rebels would never welcome him back and the archbishop... He shuddered to think what she might do if he lost her captured soul and accomplished nothing.

"Ready yourselves for battle," the lead dwarf said. "We attack in fifteen minutes."

Fifteen minutes and his fate would be decided. Samaritan pulled the black pearl out again. It all came down to this and a ragtag bunch of dwarves that had been trying and failing to bring down the provincial government for decades with no noticeable results.

He felt considerably less optimistic about their chances than he would have liked.

———

Joran, Mia, and Governor Bramrule stood in the doorway of the secure room the governor had arranged for Titus. Joran's brother remained unconscious, but he should be fine aside from a nasty lump on his head. The room itself held little in the way of amenities, just a bed, nightstand and chamber pot. Aside from the quality of the furnishings, it might have been a prison cell.

Bramrule shook his head and closed and locked the door. "I had no idea your brother had been cursed. He seemed so normal when we spoke."

"That's what makes the curse so insidious," Joran said. "Under normal circumstances you have no idea anything's happened to him, but when the correct situation arises, it activates and he becomes a danger to himself and others. It's very important that he have quiet and rest. He'll do anything to escape and contact his master."

"Never fear, Lord Den Cade," Bramrule said. "He'll be well

taken care of. Is there truly nothing we can do for the poor man?"

"No. At least not until Samaritan has been dealt with. As long as the one that enchanted him lives, the spell can't be broken, at least not by me." Joran handed Bramrule the amulet he took from Titus. "This is the device Samaritan uses to contact him. Should the worst happen and we fail to stop the beast from waking, you'll get a warning meant for Titus. I have no idea how much time that will buy you, but do what you can to get the people somewhere safe."

Bramrule took the amulet like it had a coating of Black Bile. "Is this thing safe?"

"Don't fear, it only allows communication, nothing else." The governor started to put the amulet in his pocket. "No, you might miss the message when it comes through. You need to wear the amulet."

Bramrule grimaced. "Is that absolutely necessary?"

"Let me put it to you this way," Joran said. "Do you want the first warning you get to be a fifty-yard-long serpent crashing through the city?"

"Fair point." Bramrule slipped the amulet over his head but kept his robe between it and his skin.

Pounding on the nearby stairs preceded the arrival of a youthful dwarf dressed in a crimson and gold tunic. "A message, Lord Governor."

"Out with it," Bramrule said.

"The legion has found a lagoon of Black Bile in a cavern two days' march from the memorial. General Fiendhammer wishes to know what they should do."

Bramrule looked to Joran who said, "That sounds promising. Have them secure the area and we'll depart at once. If the beast is hiding at the bottom of the pool, they can let no one get close. Make that absolutely clear. No one approaches until Mia and I arrive."

The messenger looked to Bramrule who waved at him. "You heard the man, get going."

"Yes, sir." The youth sprinted back the way he'd come.

"We'll depart as well, Governor," Joran said. "This—Fiendhammer, was it?—is a competent general?"

"Of course." Bramrule looked away. "He's the original general of the legion and a national hero. As you commanded, I've transferred the new generals to other posts in the government."

"Excellent. I leave Titus in your care." With that, Joran spun on his heel and marched out with Mia beside him.

When they'd left Bramrule well behind she said, "You just made all that up. Titus isn't under a spell and you have no idea exactly what that amulet does."

They reached the stairs and hurried down to the first floor. Fortunately for them, all the servants had been ordered out of this part of the mansion so no one would see Titus when they brought him in.

"Everything you said is true," Joran admitted. "Frankly, I have neither the time nor the inclination to explain everything to the governor. I also don't want anyone to know that Titus is helping the enemy of his own volition. If word got out that a Den Cade had betrayed the empire willingly, our family would never live it down. This way, at least no one else suffers for Titus's stupidity."

"And the amulet?"

"A calculated risk. Since Titus wore it, I have to assume that's necessary for it to work. And if I'm wrong, well, let's be honest, Governor Bramrule isn't going to be a huge loss to the empire."

"That's the most cold-blooded thing I've ever heard you say."

"I take no pride in my actions, but at the end of the day, I'm an imperial noble. My job is to save the maximum number of citizens. I'll risk one life to potentially save thousands."

They emerged from the mansion and found Stoneheart waiting along with the guards he pressed into service.

"Is all well, my lord?" Stoneheart asked.

"Yes, my brother is resting. Thank you for your help bringing him here. The legion has found something and we need to leave early. Is there any chance you can collect your century sooner than we planned?"

"I can collect them anytime, I'm just not sure the job is done."

"Get them. If the job isn't done, someone else will have to do it. I want to be on our way in one hour."

Stoneheart clapped his fist to his heart. "My lord."

With that he turned and trotted off toward the main entrance to Dwarfhome. Joran smiled at the dwarf's back. He might have to bring Stoneheart and his century back to Tiber. Clearly the man's talents were wasted here.

"What now?" Mia asked.

"Let's see if we can find the messenger that brought the original message. I'd like to know more about what we're walking into."

CHAPTER 23

The clash of steel filled the tunnel with an almost painful din. The tight space and stone walls amplified the tremendous roar of battle into something almost deafening. From his position at the rear of the rebel force, Samaritan had no trouble seeing what was going on. One of the advantages of being a human among dwarves: he never had his view obstructed.

The first wave of rebels fought with greater fury than he would have imagined possible when he first saw them in their cavern base a few weeks ago. Those sad souls bore no resemblance to the ferocious warriors on display here.

Unfortunately, fury offered little in the way of protection from an imperial steel axe and the first wave found itself wiped out in short order.

To their credit, the second wave roared in without hesitation.

As soon as the defenders were fully engaged, the geomancers went to work. Chunks of stone fell from the ceiling to crash on the heads of the defenders and a few of the less lucky attackers.

The defensive line cracked and the next wave hit the broken formation hard.

A few legionnaires went down this time and the sight seemed to invigorate the rebels.

"Keep pushing!" the rebel commander shouted from the safety of the formation's rear. It seemed that, rebel or imperial, the one in charge never led from the front.

Not that Samaritan was one to talk. But unlike the rebel leader, he had a mission to fulfill.

"The way is clear!" one of the other cell commanders called from further up the line.

All eyes turned to Samaritan as a path opened for him. Time to figure out how to summon the beast. Hopefully it took less time than the legion needed to summon reinforcements.

He sprinted toward the cavern and ducked inside. A few small battles raged near the edge of the bile pool, but most of the century on guard duty lay dead or dying. Half again as many rebels lay right beside them. If not for the different uniforms—or lack of uniforms in the rebels' case—it might have looked like a family squabble.

Samaritan pulled out the pearl and glanced around for Grub. The geomancer had no doubt ended up working with his fellow spellcasters. It seemed strange not having the taciturn dwarf at his side. They hadn't been apart for more than a few minutes since he emerged from Dwarfhome. Strange what you got used to.

He put Grub out of his mind and focused. Ether gathered around his hand and probed the pearl. He hoped for some sign of how to release the soul trapped inside, but found nothing.

Both the pearl and the magic bound into it appeared impenetrable.

Well, he'd just have to try his backup plan.

From the edge of the pool, he tossed the pearl toward the center of the inky blackness.

Halfway there it veered off and flew toward the opposite side of the cavern. Samaritan stared, unable to fully comprehend what had just happened.

When he peered through the ether, he found a dwarf-shaped ghost hiding there. An invisibility spell, but cast on who?

One way to find out.

He swung a hammer of ether into the spell, shattering it and revealing Grub, the black pearl clutched in his hand. Man and dwarf stared at each other from opposite sides of the pool. Of all the possibilities, Grub's betrayal had never crossed his mind. He'd thought the dwarf wholly committed to The One True God cult's cause. He even had one of the archbishop's amulets. How had he deceived her?

Grub broke and ran. How in the world he imagined he might escape, Samaritan didn't know. The cavern only had one exit and it sat behind him.

"Grub betrayed us!" Samaritan shouted. Hopefully some of the rebels not actively engaged in combat would hear him and help. "Stop him!"

With that he took off at a dead run around the pool and toward the fleeing dwarf.

He dodged knots of still-fighting soldiers, leapt bodies, and did everything possible to catch the traitor.

As he closed, Grub looked around, panicked. Samaritan ripped his sword from its sheath and stopped three feet from him.

"Give me the pearl." Samaritan didn't think the enchanted pearl would shatter on the stone floor, but he had no interest in testing his theory on the off chance he was wrong.

Grub said nothing, his gaze darting all around as if expecting help to appear.

They didn't have time for this.

Samaritan lunged and ran Grub through. His sword encountered no resistance and the dwarf slowly dissolved into shards of ether.

An illusion. He wanted to scream, but it would do no good.

Samaritan spun and studied the battlefield, this time with his magical sight. It revealed no sign of Grub. He must have already escaped the cavern. Where did he think he could go? None of the rebel groups would take in a traitor.

He frowned. Maybe Grub wasn't a traitor so much as a spy. His true masters might well be the imperial lapdogs in Dwarfhome. That would be the worst possible outcome. Samaritan didn't dare ask the archbishop for another pearl.

But maybe she'd help him find the stolen one. If Grub still had the amulet, maybe she had some kind of magic to find it. Such a thin hope on which to hang the entire success or failure of the mission, but he had nothing else.

"What the hell happened?" The commander of the combined rebel force came stomping over toward him. His cheeks were red above his beard and his thick eyebrows had drawn down so low his eyes were barely visible.

Samaritan quickly explained about Grub. "He saved my life twice. I had no idea he was a traitor. I need to contact the archbishop and see if she can help me track him down. Do you have enough people to hold the cavern if reinforcements show up?"

"I don't have a choice. My scouts say the legion already has every exit sealed off. We can't flee if we wanted to. Our only hope is to wake your damn monster. Do what you have to. We'll hold as long as we can." The commander shook his head. "A bloody traitor in our midst. Never would've believed it."

Samaritan dismissed the commander's grumbling and pulled out his amulet. The ether gathered and he focused on the archbishop's cold, beautiful features.

A few seconds later her psychic presence appeared in his mind. *I didn't expect to hear from you again so soon. You have good news?*

"No, Archbishop. Grub betrayed us and stole the pearl. I think he still has the amulet you gave him. Can you guide me to him?"

I didn't think the dwarf had it in him. He always seemed so defeated whenever he contacted me. Clearly he's a better actor than I gave him credit for.

"Forgive the question, but can you not read our minds when we connect like this?"

Not the way you mean. I can read your surface thoughts. That's how I hear your words, I see them in your mind as you speak. But the link is too weak for anything deeper.

Samaritan felt better knowing she couldn't read all his thoughts.

As for finding Grub, or his amulet at least, that's no problem. The amulet has stopped about half a mile from your location. An image appeared in his mind of a bright cave off the central tunnel. *The amulet is there. More than that I can't say.*

"If he's there, I'll deal with him. Thank you for your help."

The archbishop's presence vanished without further comment.

He shivered. Even her mental touch left him chilled to the

bone. "Commander, I have Grub's location. I'll return as quickly as I can."

"It better be damned quick," the commander said. "The legion won't hold off for long."

Samaritan turned and ran. He'd be as quick as possible. Unfortunately, the enemy always had a say in these things. Nevertheless, he intended to silence Grub once and for all.

———

At the end of the day, the messenger General Fiendhammer sent knew no more than what the boy told Governor Bramrule. He hadn't even seen the bile pool himself. That had been two days ago and now Joran found himself and Mia surrounded by Stoneheart's century as they approached the temporary base of Dwarfhome's legion.

The march north had been peaceful enough. Joran didn't know what he should have expected, but somehow with everything happening he thought the tunnels might be more crowded. Mia kept her head on a swivel and her hand never strayed far from the silver sword's hilt. Her tension actually bothered him more than the empty tunnels.

Still, he kept his mouth shut. An alert Mia made him feel safer than any number of dwarven legionnaires.

"Halt and identify yourself!" A unit of ten dwarves armed with axes and dressed in heavy mail stepped out in front of them. Joran would have liked to know where they'd hidden themselves. The tunnel ran dead straight and there wasn't a rock big enough to hide a single dwarf, much less ten.

Stoneheart stepped to the front. "Centurion Stoneheart escorting Lord Den Cade, the emperor's representative, to meet with General Fiendhammer."

The dwarf that spoke wore a silver badge on his helmet identical to the one worn by the guard at the government compound's gate.

The unit commander offered a smart salute, fist to heart, and his men quickly followed suit. "Welcome, Centurion. The general will be pleased to see you. He's been flummoxed about that black pool ever since we found it."

"Is it secure?" Joran asked.

"Yes, my lord. We left a full century of our finest watching over the cavern."

The pressure in Joran's chest eased. They'd made it in time.

Stoneheart glanced at Joran and raised an eyebrow.

"I'm ready to see the general, thank you."

Stoneheart nodded and they marched by the guard detail. As they passed, Joran noticed mottled brown tarps lying on the ground. He quickly shifted his gaze to the ether and found it swirling around them. Probably treated with alchemy to act as camouflage. Joran had read about something similar in the context of winter patrols hiding in the snow. It made sense that they'd have the same thing down here.

Joran guessed about a hundred feet separated the sentries from the sprawling collection of tents that served as the legion's command post. Soldiers marched here and there, sometimes in squads and other times in full centuries. No one else challenged them as they strode through the camp.

Stoneheart looked left and right before finally turning toward a large tent that flew a pennant featuring a giant war hammer. Two soldiers stood on either side of the flap and they snapped to attention as Joran's group got closer. Given the dwarves' lack of armor and weapons, Joran figured they served more as heralds than guards.

"Is the general expecting you, Centurion?"

Stoneheart shook his head. "No, but I expect he'll be pleased to speak with Lord Den Cade. My men and I escorted him and his sister all the way from Dwarfhome after the general's messenger arrived."

The heralds brightened at once and the one doing the talking said, "Thank The One God. He's been fretting for a week. Please tell me you're here to do something about the black pool."

"There isn't really much to be done about a bile pool," Joran said. "But hopefully the general and I can come up with some solutions. Would you announce us, please?"

"Right, sorry your lordship, sir." The herald stuck his head in the tent. "Lord Den Cade to see you, General."

When Mia's amusement hit him, Joran looked her way. She was fighting with all her might to suppress a fit of giggles. Hardly appropriate given the situation, but he supposed the herald was kind of funny. They probably didn't have to deal with many imperial nobles. He envied them that small boon. By the time they got this situation sorted out, he doubted he'd be envying them anything else.

"Well send him in!" a voice bellowed from inside the tent.

The herald pulled his head back, bowed, and he and his partner pulled the flap open from both sides. "You can go on in, your lordship."

"We'll wait out here, my lord," Stoneheart said.

Joran nodded and led Mia into the tent. Alchemical lights cast a golden glow over a modest collection of furniture, the largest piece being a folding table with a map of the local tunnels spread across it.

The burliest dwarf Joran had ever seen stood beside the table. Fiendhammer had shoulders nearly as broad as he was tall, making him look even more like a barrel than his kinsmen. Gray streaked his long beard and his right eye appeared gouged out. A war hammer Joran doubted he and Mia could lift together leaned against the table.

They stopped beside the table and Fiendhammer said, "Lord Den Cade. You made good time on your journey north. Word is you also arranged for my fellow 'generals' to find alternate employment. Much obliged for that. Those noble idiots only ever got in the way. No offense."

"A legion has one general," Joran said. "And I take no offense when told the truth. Now, tell me what's going on."

Fiendhammer chuckled. "You and I are going to get along fine. Now to business. I've got ten-man patrols running in every direction for fifty miles. Unfortunately, that leaves plenty of gaps for the enemy to exploit. We found and secured the bile pit as ordered. So far no sign of the target."

"Where is the bile pit from here?" Joran asked.

The general pointed at a steel disk on the map. "That's us, or near enough anyway. Maps down here are iffy at best given tunnel collapses, volcanic eruptions, and quakes. The pit is about ten miles north and a little east of here just off one of the secondary tunnels. No way is one guy getting through them all."

"How did you not know about the pit?" Mia asked.

Fiendhammer glowered at her, but after everything Mia had been through lately she just stared back and waited for an answer.

He blew out a sigh. "There's nothing out here of any value. As long as the rebels stay confined to tunnels with nothing more useful than bare stone, mushrooms, and rats, we don't bother with them. There are too many important areas, like the mines, that we need to guard."

"So no patrols in the area thus no one found the pit until

now." Joran didn't especially like it, but the general had a point. Dwarfhome didn't have enough resources to control every mile of tunnel down here. "That's unfortunate, but irrelevant to our current situation. You can pull back your patrols to within ten miles of the pit. The beast has to be hidden down there and keeping Samaritan from waking it is all that matters. We need to figure out how to seal the cavern so no one can ever reach it again."

Fiendhammer raised a hand and cocked his head. "One moment, please."

Joran and Mia shared a look. It appeared that the general heard something audible only to him. Joran shifted his vision to the ether and sure enough a little stream of magic ran through the air and into Fiendhammer's ear.

"What's going on?" Mia asked.

Joran shook his head. She could no doubt see the energy flow through their link, but neither of them heard the message the magic conveyed.

The stream of magic stopped and Fiendhammer said, "I didn't want this to get out just in case, but we have a spy among the rebels, a geomancer. He just contacted me. The century protecting the cavern has been wiped out. My agent managed to steal the item Samaritan needs to wake the beast, but he's in need of rescue."

"I'll take my team," Joran said. "Whatever he has, I need to see it. Where is he?"

Fiendhammer stabbed the map with a chunky forefinger, indicating a cave about halfway between them and the bile cavern. "You'll know him by the code phrase 'snake in the stone.'"

The meeting place looked to be a good five hours away. Hopefully the spy could hold out until they arrived.

CHAPTER 24

Samaritan crept down the empty tunnel, all his senses, both magical and mundane, strained for any sign of the traitor. He found only silence and darkness for his trouble. The silence, broken only by his soft footfalls, unnerved him.

For weeks he and Grub had traveled the tunnels side by side, facing the lava ghost and other obstacles. He wanted to punch something. The miserable coward tricked him completely. He'd saved the dwarf's life for crying out loud! Part of him cursed the decision, but another part knew that if he'd allowed Grub to die that day, he never would've found the pool.

Like as not he'd never know why Grub betrayed the cause. Certainly asking once he killed the little shit wouldn't yield any answers.

A light appeared in the tunnel ahead of him. That had to be the bright cave.

Samaritan stopped and held his breath. Still nothing broke the absolute silence.

Easing his sword out of its sheath, he tiptoed closer.

Five feet away he lunged through the entrance, weapon leading.

No Grub, but the amulet sat on the stone floor, mocking him. He knew Grub wasn't an idiot, so finding him here had been a thin hope.

Now where to search?

Samaritan bent and collected the amulet.

When he did, a thread of ether snapped and a tremor ran through the floor.

He dropped his sword and leapt as the stone started to collapse, catching the lip with the tips of his fingers. That had been far too close.

"Figured it'd be you that showed up." He looked up at Grub to find the dwarf shaking his head. "I would have preferred someone else. You did save my life, so I feel kind of bad about this."

Samaritan barely had time to wonder if this was how Antius felt before he cut the rope when Grub stomped on his fingers.

Instinct prompted him to send ether into his legs and hips.

When he hit the floor a second later, his enhanced limbs absorbed the fall without damage. Grub still looked down at him with a sad little frown. The pity offended Samaritan almost more than the betrayal.

"I should drop a boulder on your head," Grub said. "But like I said, you saved my life. Consider this me returning the favor. We're square now. If you come after me again, I'll dash your brains out."

With that final warning, Grub strode out of sight, leaving Samaritan alone in the dark again. Alone but alive. He intended to make Grub pay for his kindness.

But not immediately. He'd be vulnerable when he emerged from the pit.

Samaritan forced himself to wait a slow hundred count. As he counted, he picked up his sword, checked the edge, and sheathed it. Hate the empire though he might, he'd never say their swords lacked quality. When enough time had passed to let Grub get a safe distance away, he summoned even more ether into his legs, gathered himself, and leapt straight up.

Even with his magically enhanced legs, the jump ended up a close thing. Once again he found himself dangling from the lip of the pit by his fingertips. At least this time no one tried to step on them.

With a heave of effort, he pulled himself up and slung a leg over the ledge before rolling to a safe spot. He released the spell and gasped for breath. Between the magic and exertion, his heart raced like a frightened hare.

A few deep breaths calmed him and he climbed to his feet. Clearly, as a wizard, he was no match for Grub, but he knew that already. He also seriously doubted the dwarf would lower his guard just because he dropped Samaritan into a pit.

No, catching up to Grub and reclaiming the pearl wouldn't be a simple matter. But he'd do it, one way or another.

A glance at the ether revealed no sign of the dwarf's passing. Releasing the magic, he studied the floor. No tracks or other signs, but it didn't take a genius to figure out Grub would be heading toward the enemy, not the rebels. Should he succeed in reaching the legion, Samaritan's hopes of success died.

The tunnel didn't branch for as far as he could see.

Samaritan set out, sword at the ready. He'd have to hope he spotted Grub before the geomancer realized he'd come after him. He gave a mental shake of his head. They'd traveled together long enough that Grub doubtless already knew that as long as Samaritan made it out of the pit, he'd be coming.

He worked his way along at a brisk walk, magical and mundane senses alert for traps. Everything in him screamed that he should run, but he ignored that voice. If he ran, he might miss something. And if he missed something he might walk into another trap. He had no doubt that the result would be a boulder to the skull.

His margin for error had dropped to nothing.

Samaritan didn't know how long he followed the tunnel. It felt like miles, but he doubted he covered even half a mile given the many twists and turns. At least it hadn't branched. For all his power, Samaritan doubted Grub had the ability to pass through solid rock. That meant the dwarf had to be somewhere ahead of him. Far ahead of him given the total silence of the tunnel.

Samaritan paused and held his breath, listening to confirm the lack of footsteps. Had he passed Grub and not realized the dwarf had hidden himself with magic? It seemed impossible since he hadn't released his magical vision since he set out.

He looked back and again saw nothing to the limit of his darkvision spell.

Where was the little shit?

He caught a flicker of movement out of the corner of his eye.

Instinct and years of fighting saved him.

He raised his sword with a foot to spare, turning aside an overhead chop from a leaping Grub.

The force of the blow drove him back a stride.

Samaritan quickly recovered his balance, ready to fend off the next strike.

Instead, Grub stopped and stared at him from a yard away.

Now that his ambush had failed, he probably doubted his ability to defeat a warrior in a fair fight.

"Just give me the pearl," Samaritan said. "I don't care about you, only completing the mission. You can go about your life."

"Right, I can go about my life. As if the creature you plan to release won't kill everyone I care about in Dwarfhome."

"You can't beat me in a fair fight. If you could, you wouldn't have resorted to an ambush." Samaritan eased forward.

Just a little closer and a fast lunge might end it.

Grub increased the distance between them by an equal amount. "You say that like you expect me to fight fair."

A surge in the ether warned Samaritan, but he still couldn't do anything about it.

Grub slammed his lead foot down on the stone.

A shock wave lifted Samaritan off the ground and sent him flying six feet straight back.

He landed hard, but kept both his sword and his wits. Any moment he expected to find Grub rushing in to attack.

When nothing happened for a second, he scrambled to his feet in time to see the dwarf running down the tunnel for all he was worth.

Samaritan took off after him. It was a race now. If he lost, all hope of waking the beast vanished.

Ether surged through his legs and he put on another burst of speed. This much magic use would cost him, but he'd gladly endure the pain if it meant victory.

———

Joran, Mia, and Stoneheart's century set out an hour ahead of the legion reinforcements. They'd be traveling through smaller side tunnels that led to the place they were meeting Fiendhammer's spy, a dwarf with the rather unlucky name of Grub. That seemed a horrible name to give your child. When he asked Fiendhammer about it the general said that when a youthful Grub showed signs of geomancer ability, his parents changed his first name to Grub to show that they didn't hold magic users in high regard.

The stupidity of that hardly bore comment. Given magic's utility, Joran would have thought the dwarves would do all they could to encourage their geomancers. At least, he'd thought that for the half a second it took him to remember the church and how they considered any magic besides alchemy the work of demons. Given that, it made sense that the parents would want to distance themselves from a child some might consider possessed.

It was stupid from both directions. The empire lost valuable assets and a bunch of kids born with the dubious fortune to be wizards suffered as lesser members of society. At a minimum it explained why some geomancers joined the rebels. It also kind of explained why Grub had become a spy. If he showed that a geomancer, despite his theoretically cursed nature, could serve loyally in a dangerous post, he might buy goodwill for others of his kind.

He shoved the random thoughts away. Though they might keep him entertained on the boring hike, he needed to focus as they neared the spot where they were to meet Grub. Assuming he'd guessed their pace correctly, they had to be getting close.

"What do you think, Stoneheart?" Joran asked.

"Not far now, my lord. Maybe half a mile." Stoneheart looked back. "The general explained to you about the utility of maps down here, right?"

"He basically said they were all but guesses."

"True enough. Especially in the small tunnels like these. Out in the main passages things are more stable."

"I hear someone running," Mia said.

"Defensive positions!" Stoneheart stepped back beside Joran and Mia while his men moved forward to create a shield wall between them and whatever was coming.

A moment later a dwarf appeared from around a bend sprinting right toward them. "Snake in the stone! Snake in the stone!"

"That's our spy," Joran said. "Make a gap."

The legionnaires shifted to make a narrow aisle for Grub. At the edge of their light a figure in white appeared.

Samaritan.

He glared at the dwarves, his grip tightening on his sword. Joran doubted he was mad enough to attack a full century of dwarf soldiers, but if he did, it would make things way easier.

Joran pulled an adhesive vial out of a hidden pocket in his cloak and whipped it at Samaritan.

The fallen White Knight swirled his cloak around to protect his body. The vial shattered on his torso, but the powerful adhesive sloughed off his enchanted cloak.

A disappointment, but hardly a surprise.

Samaritan offered an inarticulate cry of rage and sprinted back the way he'd come.

"Do we pursue, Lord Den Cade?" Stoneheart asked.

"No. There's no telling what sort of trap he might set up for you. Besides, we have the item he needs to wake the beast. Fiendhammer's legion will deal with the rebels and hopefully Samaritan with them." Joran turned his focus to the still-panting Grub. "You do have the item, right?"

Grub straightened and pulled the biggest black pearl Joran had ever seen out of his pocket and handed it to him. It seethed with power and corruption in the ether. Not as strong as the black sword, but not far short. Unfortunately, Joran had no idea what it did or how it would wake the beast.

"Where did he get this?" Joran asked.

Grub's face twisted in distaste. "A corpse-pale hand dropped it in his lap."

Of all the answers Grub might have given, that had to be the one Joran expected the least. "Maybe you'd better tell us everything."

"Beg pardon, my lord," Stoneheart said. "But won't this keep until we're safe at legion headquarters?"

"Depending on what our new friend says, we might not be returning to base. The short version, if you please," Joran said.

Grub cocked his head and drew his eyebrows down. "I'm a geomancer, you know. A cursed being."

"I know what you are and you're hardly cursed. You just had the misfortune to be born at the wrong time in the wrong place."

"What the hell kind of imperial noble are you?"

Joran smiled. "The reasonable kind. Don't worry, there aren't that many of us. Now, please tell us everything that's happened since Samaritan showed up, as succinctly as possible."

Grub started talking. Most of his story was unremarkable enough. Thankfully Grub had no idea who Samaritan met in Dwarfhome. That would help keep Titus's betrayal as quiet as possible. Given the number of patrols searching for them, their successful evasion seemed a minor miracle.

"Why didn't you just turn yourself in to one of the patrols?" Mia asked. "They could have dealt with Samaritan right then and saved us all this trouble."

"I considered that," Grub said. "But only General Fiendhammer knew I was spying on the rebels. Had a patrol caught us, they likely would've killed us both and asked questions later. Much as I wish to protect Dwarfhome, dying in the process interests me not in the least."

Joran found no fault in his reasoning. No one wanted to die for the cause. At least no one outside the White Knights.

"Please continue," Joran said.

Grub didn't have much more to say. They eventually spotted the bile pit's corruption and followed it. After calling in the rebels and defeating the legionnaires, a portal opened and that pale hand dropped the pearl into Samaritan's lap. Grub stole it at the earliest opportunity and fled.

"That hand and the magic that let it appear worries me," Joran said. "Do you know who it belonged to?"

"I don't know, but I suspect it belonged to the archbishop. At least that's what she calls herself. She's the head of The One True God cult."

"Their leader's a woman?" Mia asked.

Her surprise seemed odd since they both knew Alexandra.

"She used to be certainly. What little I know makes me think she long ago became something else, something more— or less, depending on your point of view. Something not human for sure."

"She's a wizard then?" Joran asked.

"A tremendously powerful one. I doubt if every geomancer in the city worked together we'd have a chance against her."

"If the archbishop is that strong, we have to assume she has another of these pearls. Should that be the case, and she's willing to give it to Samaritan, we've only delayed the beast's awakening, not stopped it. We need to retake control of the bile chamber. Can you contact General Fiendhammer and alert him to the potential danger?"

"The message spell is a simple one. What should I say?"

"Tell him the danger won't be ended until we control the bile chamber and that he needs to do so as quickly as possible."

While Grub worked his spell Mia asked, "What are we going to do?"

"We'll follow Samaritan. Maybe he'll fall and break his ankle or something and we can finish him off."

She shook her head. "I don't want to even think of the odds that might happen."

Joran didn't either. Even more, he didn't want to think about what might happen if he was right and the archbishop had a second pearl.

"It's done," Grub said.

"Thank you. Will you join us?"

"Yes. I didn't do all this just to see the son of a bitch win in the end."

Joran grinned. He might not care for Grub's name, but he liked the dwarf's attitude.

"Let's go."

CHAPTER 25

Samaritan would have cursed The One God had he believed such a being existed. Directly ahead of him Grub stood surrounded by a century of dwarven soldiers. A pair of humans, likely agents dispatched from the capital to hunt him down, towered above the gathered dwarves.

He stared at the group and they stared back. No one made a move. Perhaps surprise rooted them in place.

The man recovered first.

He pulled a vial and threw it with the accuracy typical of an experienced alchemist.

Samaritan spun and raised his cloak like a shield. He didn't expect an explosion. Using anything too volatile down here risked a cave-in.

His prediction proved correct. A nasty, thick goo oozed down his cloak without sticking. It looked like adhesive.

He scuttled back, careful not to get any on his untreated boots.

A fight here wouldn't serve him.

Samaritan spun and ran. He'd find another way to wake the beast.

A few minutes at a dead sprint saw his legs burning and lungs about to burst. He skidded to a stop and sucked air. When silence finally settled, he listened hard.

No signs of pursuit. The dwarves must be confident that he had no hope of success without the pearl. They might well be right, but he'd take considerable pleasure if he found a way to prove them wrong.

He set out again at a less-body-destroying pace. It wouldn't take Grub long to inform his new friends of everything he knew about Samaritan's plans. Lucky for him, the little traitor only knew what he intended for this province. Samaritan hadn't shared the greater plan with anyone, not even Titus. If worst came to worst, he always had the option to flee back to the ruined tower. It would gall him to do so, but two more beasts were hidden out in the world.

Somewhere out in the world. He didn't actually know where. If the Black Iron Empire had hidden the other beasts outside the Tiberian Empire's territory, waking them would do him no good.

The muscles in his jaw bunched and he forced himself to relax. One problem at a time. He had to focus on what lay in front of him and that was getting back to the rebels before the enemy legion cut him off.

He walked for an hour at the slower pace before the sounds of pursuit from behind reached him. Despite his hopes, it seemed the imperial lackey had decided to try and take him into custody after all. He broke into a jog and reached into his satchel. A single explosive vial remained.

He'd have to be very careful where he deployed it.

———

"We're getting close," Grub said as the group ran on in pursuit of Samaritan. "I can feel his footfalls on the stone."

Joran dearly hoped the geomancer was right. He'd had all the running he could stand. The undifferentiated stone walls made it nearly impossible for him to figure out how far they'd traveled, but his legs argued for several miles.

An explosion rattled the tunnel and sent dust raining down on them. The group slowed and Stoneheart said, "Scout unit, forward. Find out what the hell that was!"

"I can tell you what it was," Joran said. "An explosive vial. Your scouts will likely find the tunnel collapsed not far ahead of us. I had hoped Samaritan was out of alchemical weapons, but it seems he had at least one left."

"If you're right," Stoneheart said. "We'll need to backtrack to a branch tunnel that joins up to the primary passage. Maybe we can catch up to the general."

"How many hours will that cost us?" Joran asked.

"Not many. The main body of the legion can't move as fast as us." Stoneheart shook his head, looking as frustrated as Joran felt. "It's the only way."

"No," Grub said. "It isn't. There's a narrow corridor connecting this tunnel to a parallel one. It'll take too long for all of us to pass through, but a small group might still catch Samaritan before he reaches the surviving rebels."

Joran didn't need to think twice. "Mia and I will join Grub. Stoneheart, take your men and inform the general that he needs to hurry. If we catch him, great. If not, we'll wait for Fiendhammer's attack to make our move."

"Subcommander Bloodfist, I'll be joining Lord Den Cade," Stoneheart said. "Return to the legion and relay his message."

A red-haired dwarf with braids in his beard clapped a fist to his heart. "We'll be there before you know it, Centurion. Let's go, lads."

The stomping of ninety-nine dwarves quickly faded in the distance.

"While we certainly appreciate your company," Joran said. "Doesn't your primary responsibility lie with your century?"

"Bloodfist is a good man. He'll have his own century before long and I don't trust this one" —Stoneheart jerked a thumb at Grub—"not to betray you at the first opportunity."

Before Joran could speak on his behalf, Grub marched up to Stoneheart until their noses almost touched. "I've risked everything to protect a city that hates dwarves like me. While you were drinking ale and marching around Dwarfhome, I was risking my life infiltrating a rebel cell and making contact with the leader of The One True God cult. How dare you question my loyalty!"

Joran cleared his throat before Stoneheart had a chance to reply. "You two can argue later. Every second lets Samaritan get that much further ahead of us. Grub, if you'd be so kind as to guide us to that passage you mentioned?"

Grub snarled one last time at Stoneheart before taking the lead. The geomancer led them back up the tunnel for maybe half a mile before pausing and pointing at a blank section of wall. A glow appeared, revealing a two-foot-wide slice taken out of the tunnel wall.

"How did you spot this?" Mia asked. "I saw nothing until the light appeared."

"Geomancers are sensitive to changes in the stone. It's a sense we're born with. Most dwarves can find their way around underground easily enough, but something about the magic makes us especially aware of our surroundings. This connects to another tunnel that intersects with this one past the cave-in."

"I'll go through first," Stoneheart said. "If I fit, the rest of you will."

The centurion turned sideways and forced his thick chest through. Stone scraped on steel as his breastplate ground against the passage wall.

Grub shook his head. "He still doesn't trust me. None of them will. I thought volunteering would change things, for myself and the other geomancers. But it's a waste of effort."

"It's not their fault," Joran said. "The church's teachings are the problem."

Grub shook his head. "You're wrong about that. Long ago, geomancers failed to protect Dwarfhome before the age of darkness. My people never forgot. When you humans came with your church, it just provided the people that already hated us cover to officially make us second-class citizens. The others said I was stupid to risk my life on the off chance it might make a difference. I think maybe they were right."

"I'm sorry for the way you and your fellow geomancers have been treated. If you're interested, when things are settled here, I can find a place for you in Tiber. Your skills and proven loyalty would be a great asset to the empire."

Grub stared at Joran as if seeing him for the first time. "You would offer a cursed being like me a place in the capital?"

Joran offered an easy smile. "The palace has recently become a more open-minded place."

"I'm through!" Stoneheart shouted. "All clear on this side."

"Of course it is," Grub muttered as he started through the passage.

"Do you really think the emperor will accept a wizard, especially a provincial wizard?" Mia kept her tone low so Grub wouldn't hear.

"Probably not, but I wasn't offering for the emperor. I thought he might work with us hunting down cultists and, more importantly, teaching me more about magic. It's not like we have to advertise his magical ability."

Grub made the trip in half the time Stoneheart needed and Joran and Mia needed even less time than that. As he worked his way through that narrow passage, Joran had never been so glad for his relatively slender build.

As soon as they were clear, Grub took point and they started down yet another identical tunnel. They moved at a quick walk, the sort of ground-devouring trot that ate up miles but didn't leave you panting for breath. Joran assumed they did so for his benefit as the rest of his companions were in far better shape.

After an hour of marching Joran asked, "Can you tell if we're catching up?"

"He's still outside the range of my magic," Grub said. "I offered this path only as a possibility. There's no guarantee we will catch up to him."

"I appreciate that. Let's pick up the pace a little. I'm okay to jog for a while."

In the end, picking up the pace did no good. The complaints from Joran's legs were drowned out by the clashing of steel.

The battle to claim the bile pit had already begun.

———

E very inch of Samaritan's body either hurt or burned. He'd been running nonstop since using his final explosive vial to seal the tunnel, forcing his pursuers to retreat. At least he hoped it stopped them. With Grub guiding them, he dared not take anything for granted. Thus his continuous use of ether to keep his failing body in motion. Of course, using the ether like that only made the eventual breakdown that much worse.

He gritted his teeth and forced the pain away. Nothing could hurt as badly as losing her. Just forget it and push on.

So he did. Mile after mile he ran with no sign of pursuit. As he ran, he considered his options and found none of them overly appealing. Basically, they boiled down to fleeing or asking the archbishop for more help. And since he refused to give up until the last possible moment, that left only one option. If she refused him, then everything he'd done so far was for nothing.

The thought of the imperial pigs defeating him in his righteous cause sickened Samaritan. He wouldn't accept it. Somehow, he would convince the archbishop to send him what he needed.

Lights at the end of the tunnel meant he was getting close to the rebel position. No sounds of combat reached him. Good, he'd arrived before the legion as well as his pursuers. He still had time to turn this around.

He staggered out of the tunnel and the dwarves on guard duty reached for their weapons. But only for a moment. The rebels knew him by sight. After all, how many scarred humans dressed in white were running around down here?

A shake of his head dislodged the random, ludicrous

thought. Exhaustion was taking its toll. Whatever he was going to do, he had to do it soon. Before he passed out from exertion and excess magic use.

"Where is the traitor?" the rebel commander bellowed.

Samaritan restrained himself from snapping at the obnoxious dwarf. He still needed the rebels and if he lost the commander's goodwill, he'd lose the only thing between him and the approaching legion.

"He escaped. I almost had him, but his magic proved more than I could handle."

The commander stomped out of the cave to face Samaritan. Unlike the dwarves behind him, he hadn't taken so much as a scratch in the earlier battle. Like all generals with a strong sense of self-preservation, he led from behind.

"I knew I shouldn't have trusted you to deal with Grub."

Samaritan bared his teeth. "And I shouldn't have trusted the rebels to provide me with a trustworthy guide. He's been with you for how long and you never figured out where his true loyalties lay?"

"He wasn't part of my cell. If he had been, I'm sure I would have sniffed him out." The commander cleared his throat. "So what happens now?"

"Now, if you have a god you pray to, I recommend asking for help. I intend to send an emergency message to an ally who might have what I need to wake the beast. If she refuses to help, we can all die together." Of course, he had no intention of dying here, but pointing that out would do little for their fighting spirit.

"Maybe it would be better to just run and try again later," the commander said as if reading his mind. "There must be a gap in their lines somewhere."

Samaritan didn't have a chance to tell him exactly what he thought of that plan before one of the rebels came sprinting up. Whatever he had to say must have been important since most of the rebels preferred to keep their distance from him.

"The legion is here. Scouts report all the tunnels are blocked. They're deploying as we speak for an attack."

"So much for running away," Samaritan said. "Hold them off as long as you can. I'll contact the archbishop. If I wake the beast, they'll be the ones fleeing."

"It's not like I have any choice," the commander muttered. "Good luck."

"To us all." Samaritan brushed past him and went into the bile cave by himself.

He settled on the floor and crossed his legs, not because he needed to meditate, but to keep from collapsing. He'd used too much energy, both ethereal and mundane. Just staying conscious long enough to contact the archbishop would take every drop of focus he had left.

The silver amulet cooled his sweaty palms. He let the ether flow through it as he pictured the archbishop's pale, beautiful, inhuman face. The chaotic energy fought his will tooth and nail.

Even as a beginner the ether had never resisted like this. His soulmate had warned him once about what would happen if he pushed himself too hard. She called it backlash and every wizard feared it happening to them, especially in the middle of a fight.

A wizard who couldn't control the ether in battle would soon be a dead wizard.

Right now, Samaritan very much appreciated that he didn't have anyone trying to kill him directly.

After what seemed an eternal battle, the ether stabilized. Now he needed to hold the magic together long enough to get the archbishop to reply. He sent a silent prayer to any listening power that she did so quickly.

Perhaps something heard him as the archbishop's cold presence entered his mind moments later. *I hadn't expected to hear from you again so soon. I trust you're contacting me to report success.*

"No. Grub escaped with the black pearl and the Dwarfhome legion is closing in. I expect the rebels to make contact any moment."

Disappointing. What do you expect me to do about it?

"I need another soul. I can still wake the beast before it's too late."

Pathetic. You wish me to give you another precious treasure to make up for your failure.

He had no time for an argument. "As I said last time, it's in both of our interests for this to work. If the mission fails, you will have lost the first pearl for nothing. At least this way you salvage something."

The silence dragged on until the sounds of battle reached him and the ether had nearly run out of control again.

Very well. But I don't want to hear from you again until you discover the location of the Black Iron Empire's capital. That is the price for further aid.

He would have eagerly agreed to anything she suggested at this point even though he hadn't the slightest idea where to find the ancient capital. "I accept your terms."

The connection shattered.

Samaritan fell back on the stone floor and gasped for breath. Had she heard his final words? He had no way to know for sure.

Seconds later four people rushed into the cavern, two humans and two dwarves, including the hated figure of Grub.

No one had a chance to speak before a small portal opened and a pale hand appeared with a black pearl clutched in its fingers.

CHAPTER 26

Stoneheart skidded to a halt so suddenly Joran nearly ran into him. The din of battle reached them loud and clear. Fifty yards ahead, the legion battled a far smaller number of what he assumed were rebels. Given the numbers it should have been a slaughter in the legion's favor, but the narrowness of the tunnel where they fought combined with the magic from a pair of geomancers allowed the badly outnumbered rebels to hold their own, though for how long Joran had no idea.

What concerned him more was the lack of a tall man in white fighting with the rebels. If Samaritan wasn't fighting, given the state of his allies, he must have something more important to do. And only one thing crossed Joran's mind—he'd found some other way to wake the beast.

"Can you see him?" Joran asked.

Mia shook her head. If she didn't see him with her enhanced sight, then he really wasn't there.

"How can we get through that?" she asked.

"I can get us through," Grub said. "But you'll have to trust me."

"Don't do it, my lord," Stoneheart said. "He might be leading us into a trap."

Much as Joran appreciated the centurion's loyalty and determination to protect him, he needed to let go of his fear of Grub betraying them.

"Objection noted. What do we have to do?"

"Get behind me, form a single-file line, and stay close. I'll hide us with an illusion. No one will see us, but if we get too close to the fighters, they'll still be able to hit us, even by accident."

"I'll go first." Stoneheart moved to stand directly behind Grub. "If he tries anything, I'll run him through."

"I don't think so." Joran nodded to Mia. "Would you take point?"

"No problem." She drew her silver sword. At least Joran didn't worry about her running through the only person between them and two armies potentially attacking them at the slightest provocation.

"Stoneheart, you bring up the rear. When you're ready, Grub."

"This is a mistake," Stoneheart muttered as he passed Joran and took up his post at rear guard.

He might be right. Joran had no problem admitting that. If Grub had any intention of betraying them, this would be the perfect opportunity. But he got the feeling that Grub's loyalty was solid, probably more solid than it should be given how badly geomancers had been treated over the past centuries. The dwarf had something to prove, both to himself and the greater community. That would keep him loyal.

Joran shifted his vision to the ether and watched a complex shroud grow all over them. He couldn't even begin to determine how the spell worked. Figuring out how the spell functioned would be like explaining to a toddler how alchemy worked. It would be a waste of everyone's time. As long as the spell did what they needed, the details mattered not in the least.

"We're going to move now," Grub said. "Slow and steady, no unnecessary sound, and whatever you do, don't touch anyone outside the spell. Are we ready?"

Everyone, including a still-grumbling Stoneheart, indicated they were. The little group set out at a steady shuffle. Everyone made sure not to stomp or shift too far from the person in front of them. Joran's muscles clenched and he forced himself to relax. They hadn't even begun yet. If he let anxiety exhaust him now, he'd be useless when the real danger appeared.

As soon as they emerged from the side tunnel, the insanity of combat nearly engulfed them.

Grub shifted their line of approach, so they stayed wide of the melee. The shouts and screams of the dying assaulted Joran nearly as much as if he were participating in the fight himself. He'd seen combat, but always from a safe distance. Had he wished it, Joran could have reached out and touched one of the legionnaires.

He didn't of course. Grub's warning rang in his head. General Fiendhammer would handle the rebels. Joran and his team had to find and stop Samaritan.

After a painfully slow march, they finally reached the cavern entrance. Inside, Samaritan sat a few feet from the largest bile pool Joran had ever seen. He barely had time to register it when a pale hand appeared from a hole in the air and dropped a black pearl like the one Grub stole into Samaritan's lap.

The fallen White Knight stared at them with a wide-eyed snarl of victory. "You're too late!"

He threw the pearl into the pool.

It landed with a little plop and sat on the surface, bobbing like a cork.

Joran found he couldn't breathe. Any moment he expected a giant beast to come roaring out of the pool. He took some small comfort in the fact that the spattered Black Bile would likely kill them all long before the monster had a chance to.

Time passed and still the pearl just floated on the top of the black liquid. No beast, no reaction, no nothing.

Joran shifted his vision to the ether. The overwhelming might of the bile pool's corruption completely blocked out the pearl's power. He had no idea if it was doing something, or if whatever Samaritan thought he might do had failed.

Mia, at least, hadn't lost her focus. She sprinted around the pool toward Samaritan.

Or she tried to. She managed three strides before the ether grew thick and a nearly blinding light filled the cavern.

Joran released his view of the ether and clamped his eyes shut. Even so the light stabbed him in the eyes and he saw the afterimage of floating symbols he'd never seen before.

When the blinding light no longer assaulted his eyes, he gingerly opened them. Instead of a cavern, he found himself standing in a blasted field filled with blackened earth and jutting slabs of broken stone. To his right Mia staggered as she finished the stride she'd been taking. Grub and Stoneheart appeared stunned and insensible.

He forgot about them all for the moment and focused on Samaritan. The man appeared unharmed, had regained his feet, and held a silver amulet in his hand.

Joran had no idea what it did and no desire to find out. "Mia! Stop him!"

Asking no questions, she lunged at Samaritan again.

Somehow, he avoided a stroke of the silver sword that would have taken his head off. Mia didn't come up empty handed. Her blow sliced through the thong that held the amulet and sent it falling to the ground. Where the silver circle touched the blackened earth it hissed and sizzled.

A second blinding flash forced Joran to look away. When his vision cleared, he found Samaritan gone.

"I didn't get him," Mia said. "Sorry."

Before Joran could reassure her Grub said, "Where the hell are we?"

Joran wished he had a good answer. In all his reading he'd never heard of a place that looked like this.

No, come to think of it he had read about something like this, in a church book. It looked like they'd ended up in hell.

———

General Fiendhammer stood in the cavern that was the center of the most recent uprising and stared down at the empty pit. According to the reports he'd read, this hole had been filled with Black Bile when they found it. He tried to imagine that much of the poison and failed. He had equally poor luck trying to guess where the hell it had all gone.

The pit had to be forty feet deep and at the bottom a black pearl rested on an equally black disk of metal. He had no idea what either of them were and the one person likely to be able to tell him had vanished without a trace along with his spy, a talented centurion, and two others that didn't overly concern him.

The disappearance of Lord Den Cade concerned him a great deal. While the humans of the empire generally didn't meddle too much in Dwarfhome's affairs as long as the iron and other metals kept flowing, losing the Iron Princess's fiancé would bring them attention they didn't want.

He scrubbed a hand across his grizzled face. He'd rather deal with a rebel army than Governor Bramrule. For the life of him Fiendhammer couldn't figure out why that idiot ended up as provincial governor. Blood ties weren't supposed to play any part in the decision, but since his father held the post, Fiendhammer assumed that helped the current moron get the job.

He'd deal with Bramrule when he had to. For now he had a mess to clean up. At least the giant hole made a handy place to dump the rebel bodies.

But first things first. "Somebody get a rope and fetch that pearl. It looks like the thing Grub mentioned in his report."

Maybe if they handed that off to whoever the empire sent to investigate, it would satisfy them. And maybe stone rats would learn to fly. He shook his head at his own stupidity. Nothing less than the safe return of Lord Den Cade would be apt to satisfy the investigators.

On the plus side, if they blamed Governor Bramrule, maybe Dwarfhome would get a competent replacement. That would turn this complete shit show into something positive.

A trio of legionnaires arrived and the smallest pulled his armor off over his head while the other two tossed a rope over the edge of the pit and braced themselves. The now-unarmored dwarf shinnied down the rope and landed on the metal plate in the floor. He grabbed the pearl and tucked it into a pocket in his tunic.

"Is there anything else you wish me to do, General?" the legionnaire asked.

Fiendhammer thought for a moment. "Do you see anything on the metal plate?"

The dwarf took a knee for a closer look. "I don't see anything."

No sooner had the words passed his lips than a flash of light appeared along with strange, glowing marks all along the edge of the plate. As soon as they faded, Black Bile started slowly oozing out of the plate.

Somehow the nimble legionnaire leapt and caught the rope.

"Don't just stand there, pull him up," Fiendhammer said.

The two dwarves at the top of the pit backed up and soon the third man rested safe and sound on the stone. He panted for breath, more from fear than exertion Fiendhammer bet. Coming that close to being poisoned by Black Bile would make anyone anxious.

"Well done, soldier." Fiendhammer held out his hand and the still-panting dwarf grabbed it. He yanked the dwarf to his feet. "Now the pearl."

That drew a wince and soon enough Fiendhammer held the shiny black sphere in his hand. It looked just like any other pearl he'd ever seen in the market only bigger and darker. Certainly nothing other than the size marked it as special.

He shrugged and slipped it into a pouch at his hip. To hell with cleaning up. He'd post a guard, a heavier one this time, and hope that Lord Den Cade found some way back on his own. Given the general's distinct lack of magic, he had no other options.

CHAPTER 27

Once everyone had recovered, both from the shock of their sudden teleportation and Samaritan's disappearing act, Joran led the way north. He didn't pick that direction for any particular reason. As far as he could see, every direction looked the same as the other. Also, given the heat, he figured they had to be at least a few thousand miles further south than Dwarfhome. In fact, the weather reminded him of Stello Province only a fraction less humid.

The blackened earth, jutting stones, and distinct lack of anything living, even plants, was like nothing he'd ever seen. Judging from the stunned, slack-jawed expression on his companions' faces, he suspected they hadn't either.

"Your mind is running a mile a minute," Mia said. "Are you okay?"

Joran smiled and tried to make it look authentic before remembering that she'd know the truth either way. "I'm extremely anxious about our current situation. Given all the dangers the empire faces, being stuck The One God knows where won't be much help."

"You worrying yourself to death won't help. We'll think of something. Besides, one of the threats is here with us. That's bound to help the empire, right?"

Joran allowed himself an honest grin. He loved Mia so much right then he hardly knew how to say it. "It does and thank you for being so sensible."

"Where are we going exactly?" Grub asked from behind them.

Joran paused and turned around. "That's a good question. I went this way because one direction seemed as good as another, but I really should have checked with our wizard. Do you have any idea where we are or where we should go?"

Grub grimaced. "Not really. There's so much corruption in the ether I can't tell what's going on around us."

"I got the same impression when I looked at it. My hope was that if we found some higher ground, we might get a better look at the territory. North seemed as likely a direction as any to find it."

"If I can stomach it, I might be able to help with that." Grub thrust a hand into the black dirt.

His face twisted and for a moment Joran feared he might throw up. After a few seconds his expression smoothed and his eyes closed.

Joran shifted his view to the ether, eager to see how Grub used it. A minute of watching told him basically nothing. The complex energy flow of the chaotic magic was too much for him to interpret. He switched his vision back to normal. He'd have to trust Grub to guide them. Given where they were, betrayal seemed a dim prospect, though from the way he watched the geomancer, Stoneheart still didn't trust him.

And probably never would. Joran had hoped to bring both dwarves back to the capital to help deal with The One True

God cult, but at this rate, he'd have to leave one of them in Dwarfhome. He found the decision an easy one. They had thousands of outstanding warriors, but someone with Grub's talents was nearly impossible to find.

Nearly five minutes passed before Grub pulled his hand out of the ground and said, "We're already at the highest point around here. A mile or so in any direction and the land vanishes."

"What does that mean?" Mia asked.

"Not sure." Grub wiped the dirt on his pant leg. "It felt like a sheer cliff. Even worse, I didn't detect anything living besides us."

"So we're on some kind of mesa?" Stoneheart asked.

Grub shrugged. "More or less."

While Joran had no real idea what that meant for them, he did know what they had to do next. "Let's keep going. When we reach the edge, maybe we'll see something interesting."

There were no further objections and the group set out again. The hike didn't take long despite the broken rock everywhere and soon enough they stood at the edge of a vertical cliff. At the bottom, the ocean crashed against the stone. A path of what looked like broken, flat-topped teeth connected their position to the next—island? maybe. Joran had never seen anything like what they were looking at and so didn't know what to call it.

"We're in a lot of trouble," Mia said.

Joran wished he had something reassuring to say, but she'd described their situation perfectly. He doubted he could conjure a more bleak, desperate place for them to have ended up. Part of him wished they'd found another giant serpent to fight. At least then he would have known what to do.

"We'll figure something out," he said. "There's too much left to do for us to die on a blackened rock in the middle of the ocean."

———

S amaritan huddled in the shadow of a towering rock formation. His body trembled from a mixture of exhaustion and magical backlash. There had been a moment when he feared even the simple flash spell he'd used to flee his enemies might not work. Now even the thought of reaching for the ether pained him. For the first time in a while, he appreciated the numbness his despair brought.

Of all the things that might have happened when he dropped the black pearl into the bile pit, getting teleported to wherever he ended up never crossed his mind. He'd assumed that the wizards of the Black Iron Empire had made their slaves dig a pit for one of the giant beasts. It made perfect sense. Where better to hide something so dangerous than beneath a mountain?

The obvious answer was somewhere else.

He knew about the bile spring under Fort Death. But he hadn't expected to find a man- or in this case dwarf-made one just sitting in a cavern without even a simple ward to protect it.

At the very least he had a pretty good idea where the magic had brought him. This ruined place had to be in part of the Black Iron Empire. Maybe even close to their capital. If he found that, the archbishop would give him whatever he wanted in exchange for its location.

Of course, he'd have to reclaim his amulet to contact her.

He leaned back and rested his head on the stone. Samaritan's eyelids felt like they weighed a ton each. A little nap would hurt nothing.

After he rested, he'd begin his search.

———

The flawless pale skin of Fane's brow crinkled as she tried and failed to contact Samaritan. An hour of pacing in her casting chamber and multiple tries had yielded nothing. Her sending should have reached him even if he didn't want her to make contact. She'd marked the mithril amulet to allow her to contact whoever wore it.

Only two things would keep her from success: Samaritan's death or him removing the amulet. While she wouldn't weep over his death, it would be an annoyance given how many resources she'd wasted on him.

Her fangs flashed when she peeled her lips back in frustration. She'd just have to accept that he was unreachable. She had a few other agents in the area. Perhaps one of them would know something.

Shifting her thoughts to one of the cultists embedded with the dwarven rebels, she tried again. This time the reply came almost instantly.

"Archbishop," the dwarf said. "How may I be of service?"

His thoughts were muddled and anxious. Something serious must have happened under the mountains.

"What's going on there? I've lost contact with the human agent I sent along with another cultist."

"If they were mixed up in the battle with the legion, they're likely dead. Three cells were wiped out. The rest of us are scrambling to relocate just in case the empire gets serious about hunting us down."

"Have you heard anything else? Even rumors would be useful."

"Apologies, Archbishop, but I've heard nothing. The battle happened far from here and our spies in Dwarfhome have sent no new information."

His anxiety had risen constantly during the conversation. Fane doubted he had anything else useful to say anyway. "That's fine. Good luck and contact me at once if you hear anything else."

"Yes, Archbishop."

She ended the spell, her frown deeper than ever. What the hell had happened down there? The rebels wouldn't be panicking if the beast had woken, so clearly that plan had failed miserably. At last, she had to admit that given her current information she simply couldn't make an informed guess.

Her agents would contact her when they knew something. Fane had to accept that until they did so, she'd simply have to wait.

Fane's life seemed to revolve around waiting on lesser beings. How did Lord Sur stand it? Especially given that every being was less than he.

Perhaps in a few thousand years she'd figure out the answer.

———

Alexandra paced and fretted and paced some more. Judging by the maids' worried expressions as they watched her from their place by the suite's wall and the wear on her fine carpet, she'd been doing far too much of both lately. Not that she could help it. When a messenger bird arrived from Dwarfhome letting them know that Joran's dragon ship had been attacked and crashed before reaching the landing area, she'd been able to concentrate on little save her worry.

It helped somewhat that everyone survived the crash uninjured. Nevertheless, it struck her as a bad omen. She'd hoped for more regular contact even as she knew neither the dwarves nor the capital had an endless supply of messenger birds. She just hated not knowing what was going on. This was why she preferred to be at the front with the army. At least then she got regular updates and if something went wrong, she had a chance to fix it.

"I'm sure Lord Den Cade will be okay, Majesty," Marsa said.

She only knew the servant's name because she'd heard Joran speaking to her several times. At first she'd thought he coddled the servants too much, then she figured he wanted to seduce her, and finally she had to admit that Joran was simply a decent guy who did his best to treat everyone deserving of it with respect.

By The One God she hoped he made it back okay. The thought of having to marry some noble asshole turned her stomach.

"Thank you for your kind words. No doubt you're right. Though he's no warrior, Joran has proven himself capable."

A knock on the door interrupted her and one of the other girls hurried over to answer it. "Messenger, Majesty."

She walked over, trying to project calm. Maybe some news about Joran had come in. Out in the hall she found one of the palace youths waiting, hands clasped behind his back. When the boy saw her he snapped to attention and clasped fist to his heart.

"Majesty, I regret to inform you that Lord Den Cade and

his party have vanished. Reports from onsite claim magic was involved. No other details have arrived at this time."

She nodded, somehow keeping her expression from cracking. "Thank you. Should any more details emerge, I wish to hear of them at once."

The boy bowed. "Of course, Majesty."

She ducked back into the suite and swept into her bedroom, slamming the door behind her. Then and only then did she collapse on the bed and weep into her pillow.

CHAPTER 28

Overseer had long since lost track of how many days he'd been marching with the mercenaries toward whatever thing caught his mistress's attention. To the already dead, time meant nothing. Since departing the imperial homeland, they'd passed through forests, hills, and valleys.

Currently they trudged through a forest of mixed evergreens. The dozen mercenaries were as motley a collection of humans as you were likely to encounter in their battered leathers and muddy boots. They carried notched and battered swords that looked like they needed a one-way trip to the smelter. They'd serve against merchants, but if any serious opposition appeared, Overseer would have to contact his mistress for reinforcements.

He really didn't want to have to do that. The archbishop was already angry with him for his earlier failure.

So far, three unlucky groups of travelers had been slaughtered and their supplies seized to feed the group. The murders also served to slake the bandits' bloodlust. These humans had a violent streak that would do a demon proud.

Overseer didn't especially care what his human pawns thought, but it made them more useful if they were content. When he first started his work, he'd killed the first human that dared complain to him, but that simply made the rest less manageable. And if he failed to properly manage his followers, the archbishop would banish him and summon a new overseer to inhabit this body.

He shuddered. For a low-level demon spirit like him, a return to Hell would be the worst possible punishment.

Overseer dismissed the horrid thought and focused. They had to be getting close. One of the humans claimed she smelled the ocean earlier. Given that, they had to be less than a few hours from their destination.

The humans in the lead pushed through a particularly thick stand of trees and quickly retreated.

"What's the problem?" Overseer demanded.

"There's a fortress not far ahead," the lead human, Hekar, said. "The crimson circle flag of the church flies over the keep. If this is the place you want to attack, we're going to need more men."

Overseer brushed past the human and peeked out from behind the screen of trees. Sure enough, a towering gray fortress waited less than half a mile away. Tiny figures in white patrolled the battlements and a massive gate made of steel and oak provided the only way in.

He opened himself to the ether and reached out. Immediately he felt the corruption inside. This place had to be what his mistress sensed. But Hekar had a point. Even with his magic, Overseer would have trouble taking such a large fortress with his limited manpower.

"Fall back and make camp well away from the fortress. I'll contact the archbishop and request aid."

Hekar wiped sweat from his brow. "Yes, sir. For a moment I feared you might order us to attack the fortress on our own."

"No, the attack must succeed and I'm not so foolish to think we have what we need to do the job ourselves."

The group retreated a good mile and the mercenaries got to work setting up their meager camp. Overseer found a quiet spot and sat before opening his mind to the ether. He sent his thoughts flying back to the archbishop's citadel.

She must have been waiting as only seconds after initiating contact her mind touched his. *Report.*

"We found the corruption, but it's guarded by a huge fortress manned by the church. I can't take it with the forces under my command."

To his considerable relief, pleasure rather than anger greeted his reply. *Very good. I'll send what you need to take the fortress. Once you've secured the source of corruption, contact me again after the sun sets and I'll join you personally.*

It seemed even a dead man could get a lump in his throat. To his knowledge, the archbishop had never left her citadel. "Yes, Archbishop."

The connection broke and a minute later a portal about six inches in diameter opened. A large vial filled with enhanced Black Bile popped out and landed in his lap. He looked from the vial to his twelve mercenaries and smiled.

Yes, with this he could certainly take the fortress. Twelve bile zombies would make short work of the defenders. And better yet, he wouldn't have to deal with the obnoxious humans anymore.

He would please his mistress and avoid returning to hell, thus accomplishing his only two goals in life. Overseer's half-melted face broke into a smile to make babies cry and women weep.

AUTHOR NOTE

Hello everyone,

Thing just keep getting worse for Joran and his companions. Having been dragged through a magical portal to a dead land, can they survive long enough to find a way home? And don't forget that Samaritan is still on the loose and causing trouble.

I hope you'll join me next time when Joran, Mia, and Alexandra's adventure continues in The Black Iron Empire.

You can find links to all my books on my website, www.jamesewisher.com

Thanks for reading and I'll see you next time.

James

ALSO BY JAMES E WISHER

The Soul Bound Saga

An Unwelcome Journey

Darkness in Tiber

Depths of Betrayal

The Black Iron Empire

Overmage

The Divine Key Trilogy

Shadow Magic

For The Greater Good

The Divine Key Awakens

The Portal Wars Saga

The Hidden Tower

The Great Northern War

The Portal Thieves

The Master of Magic

The Chamber of Eternity

The Heart of Alchemy

The Sanguine Scroll

The Dragonspire Chronicles

The Black Egg

The Mysterious Coin

The Four Nations Tournament

Death Incarnate

Atlantis Rising

Rise of the Demon Lords

The Pale Princess

Aegis of Merlin Omnibus Vol 1.

Aegis of Merlin Omnibus Vol 2.

The Complete Aegis of Merlin Omnibus

Other Fantasy Novels:

The Squire

Death and Honor Omnibus

The Rogue Star Series:

Children of Darkness

Children of the Void

Children of Junk

Rogue Star Omnibus Vol. 1

Children of the Black Ship

ABOUT THE AUTHOR

James E. Wisher is a writer of science fiction and fantasy novels. He's been writing since high school and reading everything he could get his hands on for as long as he can remember.

To learn more:
www.jamesewisher.com
james@jamesewisher.com